KINGSTON CROW

Destiny X
Los Angeles, California, U.S.A.

The characters and events in this book are fictitious.
Any similarity to real persons, living or dead, is
coincidental and not intended by the author.

Printed in the United States of America
First edition, 2017

ISBN 978-0-9995359-0-5 (Paperback)
ISBN 978-0-9995359-1-2 (Ebook – Mobi/Kindle)
ISBN 978-0-9995359-2-9 (Ebook – Epub)

Design and illustrations by Kingston Crow.

The JubJub Club!

Triple Threat

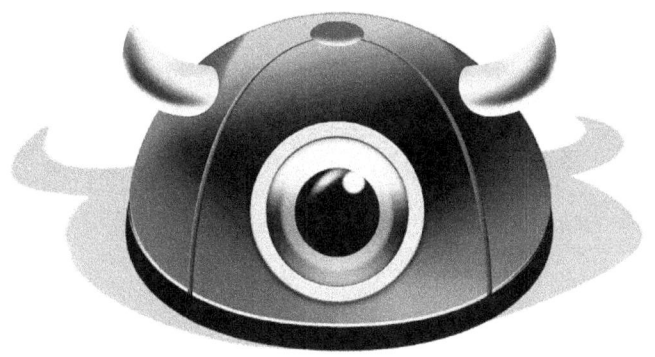

1

Twelve-year-old Harlow Banks boasted the most recognizable face in America. A leading poll showed ninety-nine percent of U.S. citizens could identify her image more often than the President of the United States or the Pope. Which may explain why they pulled a pillow case over her head, before dragging her away in the middle of the night.

Harlow sank into the backseat of the kidnappers' car, imagining the moment she would be reunited with her parents and all would be forgiven. Hands bound, she struggled to hold herself upright as the speeding car slid around the curves. The woman Harlow knew and trusted all her life held a knife against her ribs. The man driving smelled like cut grass and Paco Rabanne cologne. Harlow recognized the scent, she picked it out herself as a Christmas gift for the gardener.

Inside a diner on Vine Street, the last pay phone in Los Angeles rang. A tall dark woman rose from a red leather booth to answer the call. She wore a knee-length skirt and heels, with a matching handbag and hat. A sight to behold at six-foot-three if she wasn't a he and this wasn't Hollywood. The message was the usual and the mission the same. She hung up the phone and walked outside to the curb, boarding a Metro bus headed for Hollywood and Highland.

The gardener's car whipped down the canyon road as Harlow's mind left fear behind for something far more surreal. Her hearing became acute, and the pillow case no longer hindered her vision. Through the woven fibers, she could see the sweat dripping down the back of the gardener's neck. He turned the steering wheel hard, dodging traffic as the car veered on to Hollywood Boulevard, hurtling towards the oncoming bus. The woman from the diner braced herself as the three-ton steel shell sliced through the car, exploding on impact. The front half of the automobile landed upside down in the middle of the intersection, spinning with the engine ablaze.

A bystander ran towards the burning car, sliding to a stop when one of the doors blew open. Something very much alive emerged. The creature's scales shimmered blue in the street lights. Onlookers recoiled in horror as the wild beast cut a path through the crowd, escaping into the Hollywood hills under the cover of darkness.

The Comeback

2

Carla adjusted her seat to the upright position and peered out of the airplane window, earnestly searching below for landmarks bobbing up and down in the smoggy broth. A child sitting behind her insisted he could see Disneyland, but the park was more than thirty miles due south of their destination. She gazed down at a planet flat and infinite. No stars. No angels.

At seventeen-years-old, Carla suffered the effects of burnout from an acting career beginning at the age of two. She tried to muster excitement about the move, summoning a voice in her head, her mother's voice, reminding her again and again how this time things would be different.

Carla disembarked from the plane and floated down the escalator. Her voluptuous figure and dark Mediterranean features would have drawn attention no matter who she happened to be. She pretended not to notice the paparazzi, slinging questions at her as she walked towards a man dressed in a dark suit, holding a placard with her last name scribbled in black marker. He looked at Carla with a quizzical expression, "Ms. Shane?" Only people over fifty had to ask that question. He took Carla's bag and motioned towards the automatic sliding doors. The driver fiddled with his ear piece as he led her to a black SUV. She dutifully submitted to what felt like a thinly veiled abduction, ending her failed escape from the crazy A-list life of celebrity servitude.

Forty-five minutes later, the oppressive traffic fell away and buildings became fewer and farther between. The driver exited the freeway and turned towards rolling green hills, passing the turquoise water feature advertising the town's name in a shiny brass font, *La Fortuna* – an exclusive gated community of freshly paved roads and terracotta rooftops.

They arrived at the security gate. The driver flashed his identification to a pair of well-groomed guards and proceeded up the hill, following the graceful curves of the road. The higher they climbed the bigger the homes until the mansions reached absurd proportions.

They passed a small park dominated by a bronze statue of legendary La Fortuna founder Billy Buckets. The sight of Buckets, alive or not, always gave Carla the same uneasy feeling. Most people didn't realize he lay buried below the ostentatious memorial. Six feet under and Buckets still reached out from the grave.

The famous entrepreneur and visionary spent a lifetime building his entertainment empire. The brilliant Billy Buckets transformed a single sketch on a cocktail napkin into the world-famous Buckets Enterprises. The corporation encompassed a thousand-acre amusement park known as Starland, a Hollywood film studio, and something near and dear to his heart – *The Jub Jub Club*!

* * *

When Carla was ten-years-old, the *Jub Jub Club!* snatched her childhood away. One of six "super kids" plucked from obscurity by impresario Billy Buckets, she and fellow cast members sang and danced their way into the hearts and homes of millions of Americans.

The final day of call-backs began with the usual stomach-turning stress, precipitated by Carla's mother, Dina, holding a rolled-up script in her hand and drilling her daughter mercilessly. "They want to see a happy kid," she said, "Not some nervous Nelly who can't remember her lines. Now try it again."

Carla wore a sky-blue sun dress with white tights, her hair braided with bows, and cheeks brightened with rouge. She pulled her favorite doll from a paper bag, a bargain bin Raggedy Anne, and held it close.

Dina tilted her head and sighed, "For goodness sakes Carla. Don't you think you're a little old for that?" She hesitated a moment before relenting, "Alright, but don't let anyone see you with that thing. If they ask, tell them it's a prop, and when your name is called put it back in the bag."

Another girl, about Carla's age, stood nearby. She too got a pep talk from her mother, sounding more like a cautionary tale, leaving little room for failure.

A casting agent entered the waiting room and called the parents into a huddle for a last-minute lecture on protocol, leaving the two girls standing together. Carla introduced herself. The young girl reciprocated, "I'm Harlow."

One look and Carla knew, underneath the little girl's well-rehearsed exterior hid a bundle of nerves. "Well," Carla explained, "I'm a brunette and you're a blonde so I guess we're not really competing after all, right?"

"Um . . . I guess so."

"So, that means we can be friends, right?"

Harlow cautiously thought it through, friends had not been a part of her daily regimen. "Yes, I guess so."

The casting agent called from across the room, "Shane? Carla Shane? Over here please."

Carla turned to say goodbye. Harlow's eyes welled up. Carla held her doll out to the little girl, "Here, you keep it." she offered, "I have another one at home." Carla rarely fibbed but it seemed like the right kind of lie to tell.

Harlow caught her breath and smiled. She reached out and accepted the gift. Dina appeared at Carla's side, nudging her, "They're ready."

This time Carla entered the audition room alone, a test to see if she could handle the pressure of strangers directing her without a parent or agent present. A battery of tests precluded the audition; ink blots, puzzles, number problems, and pictures requiring her to make up a story. She figured she must have passed them all or she wouldn't be standing there now, in a room full of old people sitting in folding chairs.

A red light glowed above the camera lens. The audition had already begun, but they didn't ask her to recite lines - instead, they asked questions.

"Becoming a member of the *Jub Jub Club!*," one woman explained, "would require traveling. Would you miss your friends and family?"

Carla flipped through a list of answers in her head pre-approved by her mother Dina. "Of course, I would." she replied, "But it would be a small price to pay for such an honor. Besides, I love to explore new places."

Another woman asked, "There will be times when you work an entire week on a song or skit that gets pulled from the show at the last minute. How would that make you feel?"

"It wouldn't be the first time I worked hard on something that never happened." Carla smiled convincingly.

"And what if that song is given to another little girl to perform instead of you? Then how would you feel?"

Carla decided to tell another little lie. A half-truth really. "Being part of the *Jub Jub Club!* would mean working together. What's good for the team is good for the show."

A smattering of approval flowed from her interrogators.

"All right, all right!" A man's voice called from the back of the room. "That's enough. Everyone leave now, I want to talk to her alone." The adults seemed confused, not sure what to do next. "I said now!" he yelled, "What are you people waiting for?" They scrambled for the exit leaving Carla alone with the stranger.

Carla squinted under the spot light, peering into the darkness. An old man in a dark blue flannel suit sat perched at the edge of a chair, his arms extended with both hands resting firmly on the end of a wooden cane. He possessed a surprisingly thick head of gray hair, sporting an old fashion mustache, the kind that turned up at the ends.

"Come over here where I can get a better look at you," he ordered.

A moment later Carla was standing within spitting distance of the legend himself, the gate keeper of America's imagination – the one and only Billy Buckets. She thought she might faint.

"They say you've got it, whatever that is." Buckets

grumbled. "Why are you here? Why do you want to do this anyway?"

"Well, I guess . . ."

"You guess?"

Carla caught herself, "I mean, my mother thinks that . . ."

"Your mother?" Buckets waved his cane around at the empty room, "I don't see her standing here, do you? Spit it out - what do you want?"

"I want . . ." Carla could barely form the words, "I want to be somebody!"

"So, you want to be famous. Who doesn't?"

"I didn't say famous," Carla corrected, "I said somebody. Somebody important."

"Like who?"

"Like you."

The old man paused for what seemed like an eternity, staring off into the dark at something Carla could not see or hear. He mumbled one last time before stiffly standing and hobbling out of the room. A moment later, Dina came bursting through the door.

She knelt at her daughter's feet and grasped her delicate shoulders, "We did it . . ." she cried, "We got the part!"

* * *

The driver slowed the car to a crawl, taking in the panoramic view of La Fortuna Lake, the town's namesake and glistening center piece. Carla tried not to look, ambushed by memories of that terrible night; water lapping at the lake shore, the unbearable cold, and a stranger wrapping her naked body in a beach towel. She fought back, averting her gaze towards the nearby Santa Monica Mountains, a breathtaking backdrop tumbling down into the impossibly flat San Fernando Valley.

The driver peered into the rear view mirror, "So, what do you think now?"

Always wary of the golden goose, Carla answered carefully, "Doesn't suck."

They reached the driveway of her new home, perched on a hill, all white and sparkling. Carla had not yet finished counting the chimneys when the SUV rolled to a stop. She stepped out of the car and walked across the motor court to the columned porch. She felt very small standing before a front door at least twice her height. The housekeeper used both hands to pull it open. Carla stepped inside, surrounded by towering spaces filled with beautiful things.

"Ah! Miss Carla! Welcome. My name is Lapita. Your mother is on the phone. I'm not sure which is your bedroom but you can see upstairs, yes?"

Carla gazed up at the swirling grand staircase, "Um . . . yeah, sure."

Something to drink?" Lapita asked.

"No. I'm fine, thank you."

"Ok then, I will be in kitchen if you need me."

Carla made her way to the top of the staircase and roamed the halls of her mother's latest conquest as if strolling the deck of a luxurious ghost ship with no particular destination. The smell of fresh paint and new carpet lingered in the air. Each bedroom included a separate sitting room and bathroom with sauna. Like a dream within a dream, Carla passed through door after door, until she found the perfect nesting place, only to find herself standing in a closet larger than her last bedroom. She suddenly felt the presence of something akin to a small child at her feet. The sensation of a warm tongue licking her ankles made her do a little dance, "Jujube! My goodness, you precious little girl. I missed you so much!" Carla scooped up the warm bundle of joy covered in gray and white fur and cradled her prized Shi-Tzu. She rocked Jujube in her arms as her mother's voice bounced around the marble foyer downstairs, "Please, please be careful with that Lapita. No, no, . . . not there, over there!"

Not yet acclimated to being in charge, Dina would need time to master her new role, executing power with the arch of a shapely eyebrow and the flick of a golden wrist. She wrestled with the distinction between maid and housekeeper as the help popped open one box after another. The fact that Dina stood in a cook's kitchen she would never have to clean, confirmed something she had only suspected - new money never gets old.

When cast members of the *Jub Jub Club!* turned twelve years old, the ever-so-generous Billy Buckets made an offer their families could not refuse – a palatial mansion rent free with all expenses paid for perpetuity, provided members lived exclusively in La Fortuna Estates. Of course, that was how the famously cheap Buckets liked to pay everyone, without really paying them at all. He was a gifted illusionist, especially with other people's money.

The new mansion was an upgrade from their former residence down the hill. Dina felt the grandeur more fitting for an up-and-coming reality star like her daughter. "Besides," she argued, "the wider hallways and large public rooms would better accommodate the cameras and crew people."

Carla passed the window at the top of the staircase, gazing down at the street below. A young couple stood wrapped in an embrace, leaning against a black Land Rover. She held up her phone and zoomed in on the action. There stood the reigning queen of reality TV, Jenna Stanfield, in the arms of notorious rapper

Deadmo. A delicious slice of gossip, even for a B-list celebrity like Carla. She snapped a short video as the couple kissed.

It seemed like yesterday, Carla thought – her being the star attraction and Jenna Stanfield the wide-eyed wannabe. Jenna once auditioned to be part of the original Jub Jub Club but Billy Buckets' people deemed her too "exotic" looking – industry code for too ethnic. Carla got hired instead, launching her career into the stratosphere, only to come crashing down with the cancellation of the *Jub Jub Club!* show when she turned fourteen. While Carla's agents scrambled to pick up the pieces, Jenna Stanfield's new reality program took off, dominating prime time. Meanwhile, the *Jub Jub Club!* audience grew up, acquiring a taste for more adult fare.

Carla kept hearing Dina's mantra in her head, "Everything is going to be ok. We have options now."

Yes, Carla thought, three million of them – thanks to her father. His death had left the two of them with a small fortune compliments of a generous life insurance policy – and not a moment too soon. By then, the family had been reduced to living on what little pittance remained of Carla's salary from her Jub Jub days.

Carla trotted down the stairs and walked past piles of cardboard boxes until she reached a wall of French doors. She pushed her way outside to the patio and followed a stone path to the edge of her very own black-bottom pool. Strange looking succulents populated the garden, bathing in the heavenly glow of Southern California light. The back lawn sloped downward, allowing her to see the valley floor, carpeted with an assortment of tract homes. A large expanse of empty brown hills, once the site of a U.S. air force base, sat in the distance, waiting to be chopped up into little squares of prime real estate.

Carla turned towards muffled voices coming from the yard next door. A La Fortuna security guard shook his fist at a group of teenagers, warning he would be back if they didn't knock it off. The sound of snapping branches drew Carla's attention to a nearby hedge dividing the properties. A young man, about her age, tumbled through the bushes and into the yard. He looked up and locked eyes with Carla, clearly high on something and practically naked except for a pair of wet baggy shorts sagging below his hips. His eyelids hung at half-mast as a goofy smile stretched across his face. He put his index finger to his lips and made a shushing sound before bounding into an adjacent neighbor's yard. She remained unimpressed by the stranger since he really wasn't a stranger at all, but her former cast mate from the *Jub Jub Club!* Jordan Kraft, America's pop singing sensation, was a heavenly vision young girls everywhere summoned to their bedside late at night – except for Carla. The only vision she could summon was a twelve-year-old Jordan wetting his pants at his first Jub Jub Club rehearsal after Buckets threatened to fire him for acting like a "fairy".

* * *

A series of unfortunate events had brought Jordan into the fold as a member of the *Jub Jub Club!* Passed over after auditioning for a slot in the original cast, his older brother Brandon read for the same part. Brandon didn't really dance or sing but he was comfortable in front of the camera and easily one of the most handsome boys the producers had ever seen.

A few days later the two brothers sat on a bench outside an unremarkable office just off Melrose Ave. They listened through a frosted glass door as their agent broke the news to their mother, "Well, Mrs. Kraft, I am thrilled to tell you Brandon got the part!"

Brandon clenched his fist and hissed in Jordan's face, "Yesss!!"

"He starts rehearsal two weeks from tomorrow. Of course, there's a lot of paper work to get done and . . ."

"And Jordan?" their mother interrupted, "What about Jordan?"

"Well . . . they want to make Jordan Brandon's understudy, to fill-in if Brandon's work hours exceed the maximum allowed by child labor laws. And, of course, if he ever gets sick. Since they're brothers they can practice together, which I thought . . ."

"What did they say about Jordan, exactly?" The

boys cringed at the steely tone of their mother's voice.

The agent hesitated, nervously looking down, shuffling his notes, "Let's see . . . what's the word they used here . . ." He paused when his finger found the right place. "Well, the studio felt he wasn't boyish enough. You know, rough and tumble, like Brandon. A real boy."

Brandon pretended not to hear, staring straight ahead at the wall. Jordan knew what the agent meant but he wasn't going to cry. He was no sissy.

* * *

She heard her mother's voice calling from the dining patio. "Carla, darling! So nice to see you, honey!" Carla made her way back up the hill as her mother continued, "What in the world are you doing home, sweetheart? I thought you arrived tomorrow."

"Change of plans." Carla explained, "They decided to release me a day early."

"Why didn't you call and let me know."

"They took my phone away before I left, remember?"

"Well, you must be doing much better or you wouldn't be standing here now." Dina paused for an acceptable amount of time before turning to business. "You're keeping your fitting appointment at Benet's tomorrow, right?"

Dina gave orders by power of suggestion. As long as Carla could remember, her mother always spoke to her in a friendly but casual manner, as if an acquaintance. It seemed to keep anything too complicated at a safe distance. Carla could smell the layers of perfume and hair product – a sure sign her mother would be leaving soon.

Dina rattled off a to-do list as Carla followed her back into the house, "So, listen . . . I forgot to tell you. I'm attending a dinner this evening. I wish I could get out of it, but I can't. I won't be home until late so don't wait up for me. Lapita made some tamales for your dinner. We'll catch up tomorrow and . . . oh wait, shoot . . . I forgot! There is a meeting tomorrow here at the house. Anyway, don't let me forget, I've prepared a little surprise for you."

Dina's phone buzzed in her hand, "Oh my, Charles is here already." She quickly grabbed her purse and ran out the front door leaving her daughter behind.

Relieved to finally be alone, Carla rifled through the empty kitchen drawers until she found a lone plastic fork and proceeded to finish off the tamales. She was eager to tweet about her run-in with Jordan Kraft, but her phone was almost dead and the charger nowhere to be found. Everything else remained packed away in dozens of unmarked boxes strewn about the house.

Carla had forgotten to ask Dina which bedroom belonged to her. She wandered upstairs and trolled the hallways until she found a room with her clothes piled high on a king-sized mattress. She shoved the clothes to the floor and collapsed on the bed, holding the phone in her hand – the video of her famous reality star neighbor, Jenna Stanfield, still paused on the screen. Well, Carla thought as she stared at the frozen image, if that dumb chick can build an empire with her ass – then anything is possible. She rolled over on her side and studied her reflection in the mirror. Something in the background disrupted her gaze. Carla turned to face the dresser. A jewelry box sat on top, the exterior painted with exotic flowers and magical creatures. She wondered if this is what her mother meant by a surprise. She approached with caution, gently lifting the lid. Two small figures popped up. A man and a woman holding hands. Both naked except for well-placed fig leaves. Carla felt around the back, turning the key clockwise a few times, but nothing happened. She picked up the box with both hands and banged it on the dresser. Adam and Eve proceeded to dance in circles to a Viennese Waltz. As the last note played, a drawer at the bottom slid open, revealing a strange object resting inside. She picked it up. It was dark gray and fit nicely in her hand, heavier than expected, with a smooth flat finish.

A pair of high heels could be heard clicking around on the tile floor of the foyer downstairs. Carla retraced her steps down the hall and descended the stairs, peering into the darkened entryway, "Hello? Dina . . . Is that you?" She reached the foyer and walked towards the living room. A table lamp switched on. Carla jerked to a stop, throwing her hands up at the sight of a dark figure looming in the shadows. The woman stood at least six feet tall, wearing a knee-length black skirt, red Louboutin pumps, and a wide brimmed hat adorned with silk flowers. The stranger removed her Chanel sunglasses and placed them on the dining room table.

"When is a door not a door?" the woman asked.

"Excuse me, but…who are you and what are you doing in my house?"

The woman looked down at the object in Carla's hand, "Careful where you point that thing, dear. It could get you into a lot of trouble."

"I'm calling the police." Carla dug her hand into her pocket pretending to search for a phone she didn't have.

The woman looked at her askance, "You didn't read the directions, did you?

"What are you talking about?"

"I thought so," The woman sighed, "They never

do. Big mistake. I'm talking about that sweet little gadget in your hand, there."

Carla looked down, "You mean this?" She waved the object in the air.

The woman's hand shot up, "Again, I cannot emphasize enough – do not point that thing in my direction!"

Jujube suddenly came charging out from under the coffee table in full attack mode, barking wildly at the stranger. The lady flicked her wrist, freezing the little dog in mid-bark, then held out her hand, twiddling her fingers, "Fabulizer please."

Carla was still staring at poor Jujube.

The woman helped herself to the object, carefully removing it from Carla's grasp. "So," the lady began, "what we have here is the one and only Fabulizer. A wonderful little invention, if used correctly, that will replace your sorry ass fate for a more fabulous one. Hence, the name Fabulizer - I made it up myself. Well, I renamed it. The original was impossible to pronounce. Anyhow, it was recently brought to my attention that you desire to have the same dazzling career as your charming new neighbor - Jenna Stanfield. Using a simple two-step process I call 'point and shoot', you can easily commandeer the success of your competitor. In this case, you simply point," she aimed at a nearby vase, "and shoot the dumb bitch – just like that. Your target won't feel a thing, and if her back is turned, she will never be the wiser. You, on the other hand, will feel a short burst of energy running through your body, upon which shortly thereafter you will experience the new and improved you. Easy as pie. Right?" She extended her arm and offered Carla the Fabulizer.

Carla's eyes widened as she accepted the curious object, "How do I know it really works?"

"I turned that little pet of yours into a doorstop, didn't I?" The woman retrieved her sunglasses from the dining room table, calling over her shoulder as she sauntered towards the front door, "Just remember my dear, you only get one chance – so you better make it count."

Carla was full of questions but it was too late. She

watched in stunned disbelief as the lady drifted through the closed door undeterred by the laws of physics. Jujube came back to life, chasing after the mysterious stranger with the full expectation of passing through the front door too – slamming into a solid slab of white oak.

3

Carla arrived late for her fitting, pulling up to the valet stand at Benet's Department Store and dashing inside. She snaked through the makeup display counters where two young salesmen stood chatting. They wore more product than their female clients and possessed super-natural social skills, making them an excellent source of industry gossip. Carla paused within earshot, pretending to ponder a new shade of lip gloss as the salesmen traded classified information.

"Did you see that hideous Versace hanging off of her?" one asked, ". . . and that booty! I just don't get it. My boyfriend would dump me if I let my ass get that big!"

Carla's ears pricked up. Only one person in town fit that description. She grew queasy at the thought of running into Jenna Stanfield, the queen of back-handed compliments and public put-downs. Every encounter with the reality star seemed to end badly. Carla stepped into the elevator and tapped the 'down' button. The basement storage room included a small bathroom known only to a handful of clientele, offering absolute privacy for the discrete celebrity who wished to maintain the illusion not everyone poops.

Carla stepped out of the elevator and into a dingy room filled with stacks of miscellaneous boxes. She navigated to the end of an improvised pathway, reaching an unmarked door and entering. The restroom harkened back to a forgotten time; the floor and walls covered with black and white checkered tiles, and Art-deco lamps hanging overhead, illuminating the windowless room. A pair of women's shoes poked out from under the first stall. Carla walked to the end of the row for maximum privacy and closed the door. An uncomfortable silence hung in the air, two strangers perfectly aware of what the other was doing. Suddenly, a familiar voice broke the tension. It was Jenna Stanfield babbling away on her phone, her swollen lips sinking ships at an alarming clip. Carla panicked, unsure whether to make a clean getaway or wait until her nemesis had left. She decided to hold up and listen, trying to decipher who the person might be on the receiving end . . . an agent . . . a therapist?

"Because I say so!" Jenna snapped, "Yes, I know - but she just got out of rehab and I'm not going to risk hurting my brand for some charity case . . ."

Carla's ears burned as the blood rushed to her head.

"Anyway, it doesn't matter. The network decided to drop her pilot from the Thursday night lineup. I don't think her agent even knows yet."

Carla sat in silence as humiliation washed over her, but the tears did not come - those had dried up years ago. Her hands shook. She pulled her purse open searching for pills, only to be confronted by that ridiculous gadget. The surface registered a cool blue-gray under the restroom lights. She examined the strange contraption, entertaining the absurd notion that maybe she could indeed make everything right with two simple steps. The girl stood at the sink now, still talking on the phone. Carla took a deep breath and pushed the stall door open, approaching her competition from behind. Fabulizer in hand, she pointed towards Google's most popular search term and squeezed the trigger. The starlet stiffened as an audible gasp rose from her lungs and filled the room. The tall dark lady was right. A flash of bright light, a surge of energy, and Carla reigned fabulous again.

They're Just
Like Us

4

A soft light glowing through the curtains suggested it might be later than Carla thought. She stretched her arms towards the ceiling, then quickly pulled her hands back to her chest, sitting upright as she tried to retrace her steps. A light tap on the bedroom door and the sound of Lapita's voice placed her squarely in the present. "Good morning Miss Carla! May I come in please?"

"Yes, of course, come in. Lapita, right?"

"Yes, very good Miss Carla." Lapita held a tray laden with a banana, a greenish protein shake, and a square peach colored pill. She set the ensemble down on the bedside table.

"What's that for?" Carla picked up the pill and studied it closely.

"Don't you remember Miss Carla? Doctor's orders." Lapita gathered up stray clothing from the floor. She reached for a dress hanging over a full-length mirror occupying a corner of the room.

"No, no . . . please don't move that," Carla pleaded, "not until I lose a few more pounds."

Lapita picked up the empty tray and walked to the door, "I almost forget. Miss Dina needs you downstairs right away. She says you have meeting in fifteen minutes."

Carla brought her hand to her forehead, "Oh no, I forgot. Tell her I'll be down in a second."

Carla ignored her breakfast, digging through a pile of clothes until she found the dress with the fewest wrinkles. She slipped on a Zac Posen with teal print and hurried downstairs, her heels clicking across the marble floor of the foyer. She stopped at the entrance to the living room, waiting for someone to notice her.

"Ah! There she is, America's sweetheart," a strange man extended his arm. "How do you do. I'm Gary Rosenfeld with Blue Castle Entertainment. And of course, I think you know who this handsome young man is."

Carla tried not to roll her eyes. At least he was dry and sober this time, "Hi Jordan."

Jordan Kraft sat with his legs open and arms stretched out across the back of the couch. Even Carla had to admit he was one of the prettiest boys in the business, his brown hair combed into a pompadour and highlighted with blonde streaks. His slight stature made him appear younger than eighteen, keeping him firmly in the boy category. Jordan looked up at Carla with hypnotic blue eyes and pursed lips, just like his Calvin Klein ads, "Hey, wassup? Long time no see, girl."

Carla cringed. She couldn't believe it. The same guy who once sang Lady Gaga tunes into a hair brush now sat on her couch, buying into his own superstar image. Sensing the direction of the discussion, Carla shot her mother a disparaging look, but Dina paid no attention.

"So, let's get down to it, shall we?" Gary, Jordan's agent, pulled a stack of documents from his brief case and passed a copy to everyone. "If you look at the back of the contract you'll find Schedule C. This is the actual schedule of events the two of you will attend together as a couple. After six months, we will distribute a press release announcing your amicable breakup with the usual, 'But we will always remain good friends. Blah, blah, blah.' Alrighty?"

Carla squinted at her mother, "Uh . . . I don't remember agreeing to any of this. When exactly did we decide this was a good idea?"

Dina looked down, smoothing a wrinkle in her slacks. Jordan's agent jumped in, "Your mother and I thought this would be a good thing for both of your careers. I mean, considering your latest stint in rehab."

Carla interrupted, leaning forward in her chair, "It was for exhaustion! *Epiphany Springs* is a resort, not a rehab facility."

The agent held his hands up in mock surrender,

"Hey, perception is reality in this town. What can I say? We're trying to make things better for you."

"Yeah, that's right," Carla sneered, "better for you!"

"For everyone," the agent retorted. "For chrissake, help me out here, Dina."

Dina finally spoke. "Listen Carla, as your mother and manager I must agree with Gary. This will bring a whole new wave of publicity for you both. Publicity that would cost us thousands, if not millions of dollars - magazine covers, talk shows. Social media will light up with this story. So please, sign the contract and we will be done here."

Jordan didn't seem to hold an opinion one way or the other. He sat back with a smirk on his face, as if he didn't have a care in the world. Carla wanted to slap him good and hard, but deep down she knew her mother was right – It wasn't personal, just business.

5

Agent Gummer rang the doorbell, pushing back an unruly mop of gray hair and straightening his tie. He watched his partner disappear around the side of the house, swinging back around when the front door opened. He flashed his badge, "Is this the residence of Carlotta Shane?"

Lapita hesitated, ". . . You mean Miss Carla?"

The Agent pulled a small notebook from his back pocket. "Yeah, that's right. Carlotta or Carla T. Shane."

"Yes. One minute please." Lupita closed the door.

Agent Gummer wondered if he had been given the slip, when the front door opened again. Carla stared back, her long dark hair framing a fresh coat of makeup, "Can I help you?"

Gummer recognized her face from a poster on his daughter's bedroom wall. He hemmed and hawed, caught off guard by the uncanny likeness. Carla thought maybe he was star struck. She had that effect on men.

"I'm . . . uh . . . I'm Agent Gummer. You must be Carla Shane, the actress?"

"Yes. Yes I am."

"Well, some residents in La Fortuna say they spotted a stranger lurking around the neighborhood the last couple of nights, staring into people's windows." He looked down at his notepad, "A woman, about six feet tall, dressed in black and wearing a hat."

Carla smiled, "Are you sure it wasn't one of the *Housewives of La Fortuna*? They're always looking to stir things up."

"You haven't seen anyone matching that description?"

"Oh no, not at all. Is something wrong? Did something happen?"

"Nope, trying to be extra careful is all. I noticed in our records you've had trouble in the past with intruders . . . stalkers and the like."

"Yes, unfortunately."

"So . . ." the agent tilted his head for a better look at Carla's face, ". . . nothing like that lately?"

"No. Nothing." She paused for a moment, "You're not the police, are you?"

"No. I'm with Homeland Security."

"Homeland Security? Don't they fight terrorists?"

"Well, sometimes." Gummer chuckled, "We also protect government facilities, like the military base nearby."

"I thought the base closed years ago."

"It did, but the government still has assets in the area and we like to keep an eye out, investigate any reports of unusual activity."

The agent flipped his notebook closed and winked at Carla, "I'll be in touch if we need anything else. Remember, if you see something, say something!"

"Yes, of course. Anything I can do to help." Carla

shut the front door and listened for the sound of a car driving away before exhaling. Lapita lingered in the hall, pretending to dust. Carla casually climbed the stairs to her bedroom, refusing to display any emotion that might betray the panic pumping away in her chest.

Gummer guided his car back down the hill, quizzing his partner who sat in the passenger seat, "Ok Harris, hit me with it. What did you find?" The agent held up an evidence bag with a used tampon inside. Gummer shook his head, "Holy cow man, you are one sick puppy."

6

Carla returned home from a dinner celebrating her latest success. Her new reality show had been picked up by a major network to become the cornerstone of their Thursday night line-up. They planned to dedicate a prolific chunk of the marketing budget to re-shaping Carla's image before the show debuted next season. The sudden flood of goodwill acted as a soothing balm, healing an ego battered by the near-death experience of a stalled career. Top Hollywood executives called to schmooze and strategic relationships were suddenly resurrected overnight.

Carla kicked off her heels and dropped a pair of diamond earrings into a dish on the coffee table. She picked up the TV remote and clicked. The channel's regular programming had been interrupted by breaking news, the anchor's voice was not encouraging, ". . . An unidentified female was found shot in the basement of Benet's Department Store in Beverly Hills earlier today. The body had apparently been there for some time. Authorities are withholding the victim's identity until next of kin can be notified . . ."

Carla put her hand to her forehead, stammering to herself, "No, no, no . . . that's not right. That's not what happened." She charged upstairs, bursting into her bedroom, pushing through two more doors before reaching the closet. She pulled open a large bureau drawer and plundered its contents, searching for the music box buried beneath. The latch jammed. She picked up the box and slammed it on the counter. The drawer popped open. She pulled the Fabulizer from its hiding place and held it up to the light. It was no longer magical or fabulous, but man-made and common. Carla's hands trembled as she carefully ran her fingers along the cold gray barrel of the gun.

7

The new business partners embarked upon their first public outing. Jordan would shoot his upcoming music video while Carla hung out, playing the role of the adoring girlfriend. The studio, situated at the edge of La Fortuna, offered a perk for resident superstars – a state-of-the-art film and recording studio in their own backyard.

Jordan and Carla walked past the offices and down a hallway lined with old photos of Billy Buckets and the *Jub Jub Club!* cast members. They entered an enormous sound stage where crew members milled about. Carla took a seat removed from the action and tweeted away her boredom. A production assistant led Jordan to his dressing room, a deluxe trailer parked along the exterior of the sound stage. Jordan closed the door and glanced around looking for hidden cameras. He had no intention of starring in another salacious online video. He checked the fridge – fully stocked. A closed-circuit monitor carried a live shot of the set where he could watch the action in-between takes. He popped open a cold can of Red Bull and took a long gulp. His costume hung from a wardrobe door. He tore off the flimsy plastic covering and proceeded to dress – everything fit perfectly. Jordan gazed into the mirror and liked what he saw. He pulled the green leather jacket off its hanger and fed his right arm through one of the sleeves. He noticed a piece of masking tape on the inside collar, his name 'Kraft' written on it with black marker. It's what came before his name that stopped him cold - the initial 'B.', 'B. Kraft.' The Jacket had been part of a costume his brother Brandon once wore. That's when he heard his name being called, "Jordy!"

Jordan whipped his head around half-expecting to see a ghost. A queasy sensation rocked his stomach.

Drops of cold sweat rolled down his armpits. The voice called out again, "Jordy . . . help!"

Jordan swore he saw his older brother Brandon holding out his hand as water rushed at him from all directions.

* * *

The two boys had been flying a drone around the park that day when it landed inside the Water Temple, a large ornate well near the edge of La Fortuna Lake. The opening dropped down twenty feet to an intersection of waterways. Strict rationing required all city water features to be shut down for summer, leaving the well bone dry. It was dumb luck the two brothers decided to climb down into the well that day – the exact hour and minute the waterways reopened, filling the underground labyrinth with millions of gallons of rushing water.

Brandon placed Jordan on his shoulders as the rotunda filled. Jordan grasped the top of the retaining wall and pulled himself out. He reached back over the side to pull Brandon up to safety but froze, not with fear, but something else – something far more unforgiving. The brief hesitation proved lethal as Brandon slipped and fell into the roiling caldron of water, pulling him under and into the waterways leading to the reservoir. Officials searched the lake for days but his body was never recovered.

* * *

Carla, still scrolling through messages, heard footsteps moving briskly towards her. It was Jordan – walking as fast as he could without drawing attention. "I'm not feeling well. We've gotta go!" He grabbed Carla's hand and pulled her from the chair.

"What about the video?" Carla asked.

"To hell with the video. I'm the star! What are they going to do? Fire me?" Jordan swung the stage door open to the outside. A mob of paparazzi and fans begged for their attention from behind a cyclone fence. The young couple quickly made their way to a row of black SUVs waiting with engines idling.

"Hey Jordan!" one of the photographers shouted, "Is this one gonna stick?" He pointed to Carla.

Jordan ignored the question, slipping on his sunglasses as he opened the car door for his new girlfriend. He walked to an SUV further up the line and climbed inside, slamming the door shut. Tinted windows put an end to the show and the crowd dispersed as the caravan headed out. A young man, almost as pretty as Jordan, sat nearby. He reached over and kissed the pop star on the neck. Right then and there, for a just a moment, Jordan felt whole again.

8

Harlow was once the happiest and most carefree of all the *Jub Jub Club!* members, and the most popular too. When law enforcement officials found her, she was no longer the Harlow people knew. She retreated to her parent's house, but a full recovery never came.

Now sixteen-years-old, Harlow is a recluse, rarely venturing from her own front yard. The kidnapping had been headline news around the world, yet few details ever emerged about the tragic night. The family's gardener, the mastermind behind the abduction, died in the car crash. His wife and accomplice, Harlow's nanny, was never found. The media speculated the couple had been part of a doomsday cult, attempting to spare young Harlow a horrific 'end of times' scenario where Hollywood would be swallowed up by fire and brimstone.

Harlow did not speak following her return. She ceased to develop physically, her body retaining the delicate waif-like proportions of a twelve-year-old girl. Eventually, she regained her speech but chose to remain silent, sitting in solitude as time unraveled. Life became a daily routine of non-events arranged into a homogenous blur.

Every day the doorbell rang with a new package, usually flowers or small gifts from devoted fans expressing their sympathy for a promising life cut short by an ambivalent fate. Harlow's mother Beverly adopted a system where she would place the new delivery on a table in front of Harlow for five or ten minutes, then scuttle the gift for recycling. Harlow barely registered a response when the items were presented to her.

Beverly unwrapped the latest package to arrive, a

snow globe. She lifted one eyebrow and dropped her shoulders, "As if we don't have enough Starland crap around here already." Every piece of memorabilia served as a reminder of that horrible day her daughter was abducted and the wrenching weeks and months that followed.

The snow globe had continued to be a staple of the Starland amusement park gift shop. The size of a large cantaloupe, the transparent plastic sphere encased a miniature replica of Starland Park's space-age castle, the centerpiece of Billy Buckets' vision for the future.

Ten minutes passed with Harlow staring blankly at the miniature water-filled world. Beverly decided it was long enough. She reached for the globe to conclude the perfunctory viewing only to be met by a firm hand swatting her away. "No!" Harlow shouted, snatching the globe off the table and holding it tight against her chest. Beverly stood dumbstruck by the sudden outburst. She tried to gently extract the gift from her daughter's grip, but Harlow would have none of it, "No . . . I said no! Leave it!" She clamped both arms firmly around her new favorite thing. Nobody was going to touch it.

An hour passed and then another. Harlow sat mesmerized by something her mother could neither see nor hear. Sometimes she would smile and giggle, gazing pensively into the globe. When Beverly asked her daughter what she saw, Harlow simply replied, "Everything."

At the end of the day, her mother finally absconded with the object of her daughter's obsession, hiding it away in a closet. Beverly was grateful her daughter had shown real emotion after all this time, truly engaged and not staring off into space. It was the most she had spoken in a single day since the incident. Still, Harlow's sudden irrational fixation worried Beverly enough that she decided to bring in a doctor for consultation the next day.

9

Jordan rolled up to his house, grinding the gears on his new Lamborghini – a recent gift from his recording company. He was too embarrassed to tell anyone he didn't know how to drive a stick, so he decided to fake his way through it.

Frito jumped up to greet Jordan as he came through the front door, "Hey man, what's up . . . make it rain today?"

Jordan grabbed his crotch, "Yeah man, I just waved this magic wand and thousand-dollar bills came shootin outta my butt."

Frito and Spanx chased Jordan around the living room, pretending to catch money flying out of his ass. Jordan stopped in his tracks, pointing to a cardboard box in the middle of the floor, "What's that?"

Frito picked up the package and pulled out a remote-control handset, "It came today." He handed the box to Jordan who turned it upside down and shook it. Frito shrugged, "That's all there is, man. I swear."

The new arrival came from a steady flow of free products sent by companies hoping to get Jordan's endorsement. A single post to one of his social media accounts could make or break the success of any game or gadget overnight. The packages arrived daily, stacked up on his porch, but the novelty had worn thin. Jordan now let Frito and Spanx decide what was worth keeping. He pushed a few buttons on the remote but nothing happened.

"Maybe it needs batteries," Frito offered.

"Piece of shit." Jordan tossed it across the room.

Frito went back to watching Spanx play the latest version of *Crimson Crusaders*, swinging away at his online opponent. He held a wireless broad sword with both hands, slashing the air in front of a jumbo-sized screen as sound effects and music followed his every move. A ten-foot square mat with sensors tracked Spanx's position and a helmet allowed him to see his opponent's avatar fighting back in 3-D.

Spanx, a recent addition to the entourage, earned his place of honor after refusing a five figure deal to expose Jordan's indiscretions. Loyalty remained paramount for celebrities like Jordan, constantly thinning the ranks of hangers-on and wannabes.

The players traded verbal threats, transcribed into scrolling text at the bottom of the screen for everyone to read. A selfie of Spanx's opponent sat in the bottom right-hand corner of the monitor. Frito pointed to the photo, "Hey, I think I know that guy. Didn't he deliver pizza here once?"

* * *

Frito held the record for knowing Jordan the longest. They were both ten years old when Frito showed up to the house with his mother Marta, the Kraft family's housekeeper. It was a school holiday and she couldn't afford a babysitter. Frito had recently arrived in America and spoke almost no English. Unfamiliar with American television, he had no idea the boy he just met was a pop culture sensation.

By now fame had warped Jordan's young mind, skewing his judgment, making it difficult to distinguish between friends and sycophants. Frito's friendship afforded him the anonymity he needed to feel normal again, at least while they were together.

Jordan invited Frito to live with him a little over a year ago, after his mother Marta passed away. He was thrilled to have Frito's company. Mornings had been lonely ever since Jordan cut all business ties with his parents. As part of the agreement, he bought each of them a house. A thirty-minute drive from La Fortuna, sixty in traffic.

It wasn't long before the excitement of having a new roommate waned. Despite the six bedrooms and eight bathrooms, the situation became claustrophobic. The two young men clashed on a regular basis. Jordan tried to be understanding. After all, it was Frito who found his mother dead on Jordan's kitchen floor. She was in the middle of putting a Band-Aid on a rattlesnake bite when she succumbed to shock. In the days and months that followed, Frito's behavior seemed to morph into something beyond normal grief. He changed. Not just his personality but physically too. At first, he didn't like his nose – too wide. So, he used the money his mother had left him and had it altered, streamlined like Jordan's. Then came another surgery for the cheekbones, and then the chin. Soon the two boys looked like brothers, and at certain angles, like twins. Social media buzzed with rumors and innuendo, suggesting Frito and Jordan might be more than just friends.

* * *

Frito spent the remainder of the day trying not to touch his face, recovering from his latest procedure. He wandered around the house in a fog of painkillers with his head wrapped in bandages, eventually settling down by the pool to watch Spanx do cannonballs off the roof. Jordan lay stretched out on the living room couch, reading coverage for a script his agent was pushing – another raunchy teen comedy scheduled for summer release. Regardless of the plot, Jordan always played himself and his lawyers always made sure he got the lion's share of the backend.

Electronic chimes tinkled, drawing Jordan's attention across the room. Spanx's cannon balls had shaken the giant monitor from its sleep, displaying the *Crimson Crusaders* interface. A request popped up on the screen, "Hey Jordan, wanna play?" It was the pizza guy. Jordan had pretended not to recognize him when Frito pointed to his picture earlier. He remembered the young man too, but not for his pizza. Jordan looked around, making sure Frito and Spanx were nowhere in sight before answering, "Sure. Where do you want to meet?"

"The War Room . . . midnight, tonight."

10

Harlow's mother answered the front door, welcoming the esteemed Dr. Doug into her home. He wasn't exactly what Beverly had expected. He looked older than the photo on his book cover, dressed in Versace and smelling like Polo – his three-day stubble more like five. Beverly's eyes danced across his belt buckle. "I have all your books," she gushed, "*What's Your Problem?* and *Its Only Blood!* Very inspiring, you know?" Her nose wrinkled when she smiled.

The Doctor sat down on the couch next to Beverly and looked into her eyes. "So, tell me . . . where would you like to start?" He tapped her on the knee with two fingers.

Beverly got goose bumps. Approaching fifty, the

doctor still had a solid hairline and flat stomach – his teeth bleached a pearly blue-white. Beverly tilted her head and sighed, "Well, as you may know by now, Harlow has not spoken much since the incident. Then yesterday she received this gift in the mail, this snow globe. She fixated on it for hours. The good news is, she seemed to step out of her own little world for the first time in years." Beverly's eyebrows lifted, "I saw how you helped those other two young actresses. I was hoping you could do the same for my daughter, maybe have a little chat with her and tell me what you think."

Beverly led the Doctor into the adjacent room where her daughter sat at a round mahogany table. Harlow peered into the globe, rocking her doll in her arms. Beverly spoke in an upbeat tenor, hoping to bring Harlow out of her shell. "Here she is Doctor. Harlow, you remember Dr. Doug, don't you? From *The Ellen Show?*" Beverly shrugged at Harlow's disinterest. "Well, I'll leave you two alone then." Beverly gave the doctor an upside-down smile, mugging defeat, then trotted off to make phone calls.

"Well," the Doctor smiled, "I guess it's just you and me now."

Harlow didn't speak.

"Your mother tells me you had a real breakthrough yesterday, care to talk about it?" He paused, waiting for an answer. "That's a very pretty snow globe you have there. I wish you could tell me what you see inside." The doctor paused again, "Maybe it would help if you just looked at me."

"I am looking at you . . ." Harlow answered, gazing into the globe, ". . . in here."

"Yes, I see my reflection too, sweetheart."

". . . She's crying."

The doctor moved closer to Harlow. "Pardon me, honey. What's that you say?"

"Jub-Jub is crying." Harlow looked up at the Doctor, "Why is Jub-Jub so sad?"

The Doctor's neck turned a peculiar shade of red. He placed his hand on Harlow's shoulder. She could feel his cold fingers touching her neck. He looked around the room, lowering his voice, "Any more talk like that and I might have to recommend the same for you." He waited for the words to sink in. "You don't want to go back there again, do you?"

Harlow remained silent.

Still not satisfied he had communicated properly, the good Doctor leaned down and whispered into his young patient's ear, "I mean, after all, we're all on the same side – right?"

Harlow barely blinked, remaining perfectly still until he was gone.

11

Jordan wasn't used to standing in line but that's what normal people did, and tonight he was one of them. He carried Frito's driver's license in his back pocket in case they asked for I.D. Frito didn't mind because Frito didn't know. Jordan took a risk showing up alone. No security. No entourage. Nothing to protect him from overzealous fans if recognized. He wore a hoodie, sunglasses, and long sleeves to hide his tattoos. If anyone told him he looked like Jordan Kraft, he would just smirk and act insulted.

It was almost midnight. A couple of hours ago Jordan sat on his couch nodding off, now here he stood, excited to see the inside of *The War Room*. He always wanted to check out the night club but his fame and fans made it impossible. The club attracted people from all over Los Angeles. Straight, gay, Latino, Asian, black, white, and everything in between. After 1:00 a.m. on a Friday night, the dance floor turned into one hot mess and Jordan couldn't wait.

The ticket line undulated forward, a sluggish centipede four people wide. Jordan could smell the inside of the club wafting out of the open doorway, an intoxicating mix of sweat and cologne. Adrenaline coursed through his veins in anticipation of the evening, wondering if he would make that allusive connection, something more than physical this time. But Jordan knew better. Even if he found what he longed for, it could never go beyond that night. The last time he let his guard down, he almost lost everything.

* * *

Officer Benny Kraft was the son of a son of a cop, known for two things; being the father of Jordan Kraft, and never doing anything halfway. The latter got him through two tours of duty in Afghanistan. He was indispensable as a soldier, fearless and unencumbered by consequences. A man of action. But when Benny returned stateside and joined the police force, he was expected to be a diplomat, not a warrior. His old-school methods went unappreciated and he was forced to resign or face charges for beating a well-known pimp half to death. It was no coincidence that Officer Kraft's son Brandon drowned only two weeks prior to the incident, but no defense either. Billy Buckets' lawyers were granted a request to have all related court documents sealed. The story never went public. When the dust settled, Buckets hired Jordan's father as a security guard at La Fortuna Estates. It was Buckets' way of keeping an eye on a loose cannon while protecting his investment from further scandal.

Benny Kraft also happened to be the son of a son of an alcoholic, and when things went south, he would raise a glass and drink to misfortune. When his parents separated, Jordan's manager rented a modest home for

Benny in Sylmar, not far from where Jordan and his mother lived in La Fortuna – an offer Benny Kraft perceived as an insult but was in no position to decline.

One night, Benny strolled into his neighborhood bar. The regulars all looked at him funny. A TV mounted on the wall was tuned into a Hollywood gossip show, airing a video of teen pop star Jordan Kraft kissing another boy on the balcony of the Marriot Beverly Hotel. At least, that's what it looked like. Hard to tell, a jerky camera shot of two shadowy figures backlit. But by the time a crack team of journalists finished spewing twenty prime time minutes of innuendo and conjecture, there was barely any doubt left in the bar.

Benny Kraft checked his wallet for the gate pass he lifted from one of Jordan's maids, then threw back one last bourbon before storming out of the bar.

Thirty-five minutes later Benny stood at Jordan's front door. He had to close one eye to get the key into the lock. As he climbed the darkened stairs his anger spiraled into rage. He swung the bedroom door open and ripped the covers off Jordan's bed, "You little shit!"

he screamed. "You goddamn little shit . . . I'm gonna beat that Hollywood bitch right out of you!"

Jordan shielded himself with a pillow, yelling, "It wasn't me! It wasn't me! It was J. J., he did it!"

Benny swayed back and forth, holding his fist in the air, ready to strike, "What the hell are you talking about?" He wanted to believe more than anybody it wasn't true.

"J.J. put the video on YouTube and told everyone it was me. He was jealous!"

"What the hell are you talking about?"

"I got a recording deal and he didn't . . . now he's pissed."

Benny turned his back to Jordan and punched a hole into the drywall. "You better not be lying to me boy or I'll beat the living crap outta you!" He stumbled out of the room and down the stairs as Jordan's mother quietly watched through a crack in her bedroom door.

* * *

Jordan looked up as the line lurched ahead. Somebody stamped his hand and corralled him into the club. He was glad to be inside, where faces melded together in the dark and the pounding music made it impossible to talk. His phone vibrated with a new message, "Got a private booth . . . third from the right."

Jordan walked towards the far wall, weaving through the dance floor. Nobody seemed to recognize him. He was free and clear. Red velvet curtains shrouded each booth in privacy, a barrier to the unwashed masses pushing and shoving on the dance floor. He reached his destination. A hand pulled the curtain aside and a young man invited Jordan to enter. The pop star looked around one last time before ducking inside.

12

Harlow tip-toed downstairs as Beverly and her husband slept. She unlocked the storage closet and retrieved the Starland snow globe, setting it down on the coffee table and leaning in for a closer look at a cloud of iridescent blue liquid swirling around the plastic castle. The longer she stared the more she learned. The images filled her scope of vision, sucking her into a distant world where a tale of epic proportions unfolded. She looked dead-ahead at a future infinite and breathtaking.

The electric blue light receded from Harlow's vision, shrinking to a single point of light bouncing off the surface of the sphere. She understood now, locking the globe back in the closet and placing the key under a nearby lamp. She prodded the couch cushions for her Raggedy-Ann and slipped outside.

Harlow could see La Fortuna Lake from her back lawn, the surface glistening under the moonlight. She followed a trail leading to the shore where she climbed a small jetty of rocks and peered down into the water. She could see it now, wedged between two large boulders – the size of a minivan, streaked with red and yellow paint.

Sensing she was not alone, Harlow looked up. There, across the water, on the other side of the lake stood Jub-Jub – as close as Starland's mascot ever got to anyone. Trust issues, Harlow had been told. The old Jub-Jub, a sweaty middle-aged man, was usually found pacing outside the studio – holding his head in one hand while smoking a cigarette with the other. He was gross, Harlow remembered, but this Jub-Jub was different – always funny and kind, she never hurt anyone.

Harlow looked down into the murky depths of the

lake one last time and gazed upon the sunken relic, wondering how long it had been there. She looked up again and waved goodbye to Jub-Jub. It was time to go.

13

Jordan lay on the cold wet pavement, his side numb, wearing only a pair of dirty blue hospital scrubs. The moon shined down from an opening above, bright enough to cast a shadow. He brought his knees up to his chest and rolled over onto all fours. The floor smelled like a sewer. He forced himself into a standing position, his legs almost buckling under the weight. Twenty feet above, a large circular opening with pillars supported a concrete cupola. It took Jordan a moment to decipher where he was standing, at the bottom of the La Fortuna water temple. He looked down and gave his half-naked body a good once over. Not too bad, he thought, just a little banged up.

Six different tunnels intersected at the bottom of the well, radiating outward. Jordan could not tell north from south, let alone, up from down. Panic sank its teeth into his chest as a voice echoed through the underground chambers, "Jordy . . . this way!"

Jordan staggered from one tunnel opening to the next, struggling to discern the direction of the voice. He heard it again, "Down here Jordy!"

He saw a flicker of orange and followed the light, trudging through ankle deep water, calling out in a voice strained and hoarse, "I'm here!"

A low guttural sound bounced through the empty waterways, growing to a fevered pitch as it reverberated through the darkness. Jordan ran faster, until he found himself standing at the edge of a precipice, shielding his eyes from the rising sun shooting across the surface of the lake sloshing below. He climbed around the mouth of the pipe and up a steep incline, squeezing through a hole in the cyclone fence circling the lake. Sudden violent spasms doubled him over, emptying the contents of his stomach on to a service road. An abundance of foul smelling liquid made him heave even more. The splatter of iridescent blue vomit shimmered in the morning light.

The short blast of a siren made Jordan jump back. He steadied himself against a small oak tree, looking up. A La Fortuna patrol car rolled to a stop, communicating through a loud speaker, "Sir, are you in need of assistance?"

Jordan nodded and mumbled to himself, "What do you think, asshole?" careful not to let go of the tree.

The security officer got out of her car and walked towards Jordan. Hands on hips, she gazed down at his ashen face, "You don't look so good, honey. What happened?"

Not about to tell the truth, Jordan went with a more palatable excuse, "I got pranked by friends last night. Can you give me a ride home?"

The officer nodded, "Sure thing honey, hop in." She adjusted her rear-view mirror for a better look at her passenger, "Oh sweet mercy, you're Jordan Kraft, aren't you?"

Jordan winced, "Yes, ma'am."

"Well, don't you worry honey, your secret is safe with me. There's nothing I hate worse than a tattletale. My lips are sealed."

Jordan's new best friend continued to over-share for the remainder of the drive.

The officer pulled up to Jordan's house and dropped him off. Half way to the front door, he turned and watched the officer back down the driveway, waving goodbye as she twiddled her fingers.

Jordan dug through a nearby Flower pot for the house key, unlocking the front door, and pushing his way inside. He walked past fast-food containers and empty beer bottles scattered across the living room floor, sliding his hands along cream colored walls until he felt a door jam and turned left. He laid down on his bed and tried to sleep, but his mind kept racing. He got up and held his arms out, searching for solid objects blocking his path to the bathroom. He flipped on the light switch and glanced at the mirror slathered with posters. David Bowie stared back – so did Morrissey, and Lady Gaga too. He splashed his face with water and tried to wash away the taste of blue vomit, then meandered down the hallway into the kitchen where he poured himself a cup of coffee. He flinched at the sight of stained bandages piled on the counter. Outside, Frito paced back and forth along the edge of the pool in his favorite Superman pajama bottoms.

Jordan slid the glass door open and stepped outside. A mist hung over the hills. The white noise of the day had not yet descended upon the canyon. He watched Frito stop and bow in deference to his reflection on the water. Jordan marveled at his friend's face, no signs of bruises or discoloration - a perfect replica worthy of Madame Tussaud's. It suddenly occurred to him that Frito never once asked for his permission. Jordan felt something stir inside, bubbling to the top. It was no longer about love, but supply and demand - and there was only room for one Jordan Kraft.

14

Ten round tables filled the living room, set for an impromptu luncheon organized by Harlow's mother Beverly. Word spread of her daughter's burgeoning psychic ability, piquing the interest of La Fortuna's elite residents. Never one to overlook a potential revenue stream, Beverly threw the event together as a showcase for her daughter's new-found talent.

With little time to prepare, Beverly dipped into her party planning file from last year's *Women Who Rule* awards luncheon. The guest list included a children's book author, a daytime talk show host, Hollywood industry types and a collection of La Fortuna trophy wives. Many of the guests lived only blocks away, yet a valet service kept busy parking luxury sedans for the first hour. The living room glowed with pastel dress suits and tasteful gold jewelry. The caterers served hors d' oeuvres as Beverly welcomed her esteemed guests to her twenty-room estate. Everyone understood the day's proceedings would not come cheap. Prior to the reception, Beverly shared the going rate for a private reading with Harlow. She estimated the total take for the afternoon would be around sixty thousand dollars.

Harlow remained cloistered in a large sitting room off the main entry hall. She sat on a gilded throne Beverly rented from Hollywood Star Props, the red velvet cushions still warm from a Kanye West photo shoot. A freelance screenwriter supplied Harlow with scripted responses to her clients' most common questions. No longer twisted into a top knot, her hair flowed across her shoulders, curled and styled with blonde highlights. She wore makeup for the first time in years. Beverly had positioned her daughter behind a round table draped in purple velvet, with the snow globe mounted dead center. It was the start of something big and Beverly was determined to keep a short leash on her new venture.

Harlow now ruled supreme as the star attraction in a room filled with prominent and successful women, unaware she existed until only a few days ago. Most of them came for a sneak peek into the second act of their privileged lives. Each guest brought a personal item Harlow could hold in her hands, a conduit into her clients' private lives. The women chatted away with anticipation at what their future might hold.

One by one, Beverly's assistant led the eager women into the sitting room for a private consultation with Harlow. Beverly stationed herself not far from the door where the customers would exit when done. The results were varied and alarming. One woman, the children's book author, appeared shaken and pale after her meeting with Harlow. She asked for a glass of water and the keys to her car. Harlow's next client, the young wife of an elderly billionaire, emerged from the room smiling. A strange reaction, she thought, for someone who learned their beloved would soon meet his demise.

Harlow grew weary as the afternoon dragged on. In

between readings, she would study the long shadows falling across the carpet, looking forward to the evening when she would sneak away and commune with the peaceful lake glittering under the moonlight.

She looked up as a tall dark woman, dressed in peach Chanel and white pumps, entered the room unannounced – taking a seat at the table. The visitor crossed her long legs, gripping the arms of the chair. She directed a knowing gaze at Harlow, the uncomfortable silence a greeting between two old friends.

"What are you doing here?" Harlow whispered.

"Who do you think gave you that fancy crystal ball?"

"You?" Harlow swallowed, "Why?"

"I thought it would be best if you prepared for the future." The lady gestured to the next room, "Of course, I underestimated your mother's . . . shall we say, resourcefulness." She pulled a cigarette from her purse and flicked open a diamond studded lighter, sending smoke swirling into the air.

"You can't do that in here."

The woman exhaled and smiled. "Second-hand smoke is the least of your problems my dear."

Harlow looked away.

The lady threw her head back in exasperation, "Oh please, you knew this day would come, but did you prepare? No. You just sat there like a zombie hoping a miracle would save you." She crossed her legs the other way and straightened her back, knocking the cigarette ashes to the floor. "So, listen up. The time has come for you to pull it together. Here . . ." She slid a small square envelope across the table to Harlow. "It doesn't look like much, but it'll get the job done."

Harlow peeked inside, before slipping the envelope into her pocket.

"She'll be here any minute. You remember what to say, right?"

Harlow nodded.

"That's a question. Yes or no?"

"Yes, ma'am."

"Alright then . . ." The woman stood, sliding her clutch into the crook of her arm. She turned and walked to the door, pausing to reflect as she placed one hand on her hip and looked up to the heavens, delivering a recitation more sideshow than Shakespeare, "Rue to thee who enters me . . . for I am the door of perception."

Harlow blinked and the lady was gone.

A moment later Harlow heard a light tap on another door, the one leading to her mother's office. "Yes?" she called out, "Come in."

Her mother had been checking in all day, asking questions, coaching, and otherwise keeping tabs on her investment. To Harlow's surprise, two strange men wearing dark suits and ear pieces entered the room. One of them held up what looked like an iPhone, scanning the room. The other addressed her in a polite manner, "We'll just be a moment ma'am."

The two men nodded to each other in agreement before slipping out of the room.

The door opened again. This time a woman entered wearing a far more elegant look than the Carmen Sandiego ensemble flaunted by her last guest. She wore sunglasses and what Harlow suspected was a very expensive wig made from human hair, a shade of brown ill-suited for the woman's pale complexion. The guest sat in a chair opposite Harlow grasping her purse with both hands. "Oh, yes." She pointed a finger in the air, "I was to bring something personal." She extracted an item from inside her purse and laid it on the table. Harlow recognized it right away, her stepfather wore them all the time – a tie clip.

"It's my husband's. I'm here for him."

Harlow picked up the gold-plated tie clip for closer inspection. The front displayed an eagle with wings spread wide. She closed her hand around the object and drew a deep breath. What she was about to tell the woman was a lie, but when she gazed into the globe, she could see it would soon be true.

15

Carla struggled to fix her makeup, fighting the road for control of her mascara brush. She let her eyes stray for a millisecond to catch a glimpse of spotlights scanning the night sky – the spectacle at least half a mile away and closing in. Jordan sat at the opposite end of the back seat in deep thought, silently staring out the window.

The roar of the crowd signaled their arrival. They both sighed with resignation at the prospect of another long evening posing as the loving couple. The humiliation of yet another public appearance with her fake boyfriend ran through Carla like a steel spike. At least they shared one thing in common, she thought, neither one of them wanted to be there.

The driver jumped out of the car and ran to the passenger side, opening the door with military precision. The two young stars avoided eye contact with each other as they held hands and smiled at the spectators in the bleachers.

The event, a televised talent competition and fundraiser rolled into one, benefitted the Buckets Legacy Fund. One of the most prestigious affairs in Hollywood, the celebration garnered more television viewers than the *Golden Globes*. The program replaced the defunct *Jub Jub Club!* as the studio's way of discovering fresh faces poised for the Hollywood slaughter house.

As usual, the paparazzi and press crossed the line with questions running afoul of good taste. Carla could feel her publicist's hand on the small of her back steering her through a packed maze of interviewers, fashion shoots, and shoe cams. This was where the real work of being a celebrity got done, in the harsh light of an unbridled media frenzy. Anything could happen and did, awkward moments captured as fodder for the following day's gossip blogs; tripping on the red carpet, a wardrobe malfunction, or remarks taken out of context. You are remembered for things you had no control over. A fumbling producer spills his drink down your back and somehow you become the sloppy drunk. None of it made sense. That's why the publicists and agents got the big bucks for doing what they do best – damage control.

Carla crossed the finish line and entered a lobby buzzing with Hollywood royalty. Jordan abandoned her, disappearing into the crowd. Carla would normally be apprehensive about interacting with so many stars, but tonight she was in no danger of being approached. Despite being famous in a hundred different countries for being herself, Hollywood expected her to bring one thing to the table she did not have – talent.

Carla was about to seek refuge in the women's powder room when she saw something unexpected. She felt herself blush under a light coat of bronzer. He was a man now, tall and broad shouldered with features more chiseled than she remembered. Well-wishers gathered around him, congratulating the young musician on his recent Grammy win. Carla averted her eyes.

The last time she saw Troy Hatch they were only kids, and far too young to be so in love. Of course, the studio managed to exploit their budding romance for the sake of the *Jub Jub Club!* program ratings. The studio executives insisted the young stars wear purity rings as proof of their chastity. Over time the relationship became too intense for the program's wholesome image and Billy Buckets ordered them to end it.

Carla looked up for one last glimpse of Troy to find him standing before her with open arms, "Carla?"

"Troy!" She made a failed attempt to mask her excitement, "I didn't expect to see you here."

He took her hand and kissed her cheek, spinning her around for a better look, "Wow! You look great . . . I mean, you're totally grown up! You look fabulous!"

Carla couldn't help noticing he was still holding

her hand. "Well, I guess we've both grown up. My goodness, what are you, six-foot-two?"

"Six-foot-three, but who's counting, right? I thought I was never going to get past five feet. I was so short they wouldn't even let me ride the Willy Wringer. Remember that? I was so mad!"

"I know, I think we were the same height the last time I saw you."

Troy glanced around. "So, are you here with anybody tonight?"

"Oh yeah, I almost forgot. I came with Jordan."

"Jordan? You mean Jordan Kraft?" Troy sounded incredulous. "Correct me if I'm wrong, but I thought Jordan was . . . um, you know . . ."

"Oh right!" Carla rolled her eyes, "I wouldn't know about that. This whole dating thing is Dina's crazy idea."

It was Troy's turn to roll his eyes now, "Of course, good old Dina. How is the dragon lady, anyway?" They both laughed even harder this time, causing more than a few heads to turn.

A gong sounded and guests filed into the auditorium.

"Well," Carla sighed, "I guess the show must go on."

Troy felt a sudden sense of urgency as Carla slowly slipped away. "Hey, we should get together soon. You know, talk about old times or . . . I don't know . . . just talk."

"I'd like that. I mean, that would be wonderful. Yes, absolutely!"

"Ok then, I'll have my people call your people and set it up. It'll be great!" Troy brimmed with excitement, almost knocking over a two-time academy award winner. He looked back at Carla with a sheepish grin, waving goodbye as the crowd carried him away.

Carla took her seat next to Jordan as the theatre lights dimmed, her head still buzzing from the surprise reunion. For the first time in ages, she felt something akin to joy. She grabbed Jordan's hand and squeezed, "Isn't this a great night?"

Jordan looked at her with guarded suspicion, "You

do know you shouldn't mix meds with alcohol, right?"

Carla threw his hand back in his lap, "Jordan, you're such a jerk."

Applause spread through the auditorium as a monitor descended over the stage. An image of the late Billy Buckets, founder of Buckets Enterprises, illuminated the screen. Every year editors threw together film footage as an homage to the legendary entertainer and visionary – the usual story with a slightly new spin. Respected for his contribution to filmed entertainment, Buckets had been vilified as a quack when it came to his role as a science and technology entrepreneur. Yet, there he stood before his greatest achievement – the Starland time capsule. Each of the young stars of the popular Jub Jub Club Show had been asked to place a personal keepsake inside the vessel bound for the great beyond. The bullet shaped hull measured ten feet long and five feet in diameter, painted bright red with the words "Starland Express" written in a cartoonish yellow script along the side. The capsule would be part of a larger craft adorned with solar panels and hi-tech gadgets to be loaded on to the end of a booster rocket ten stories high.

Buckets greeted the audience with characteristic charm, as if alive and well somewhere not too far away. His eyes twinkled under the klieg lights as he described his utopian vision for the future:

"Hello, and good evening. My name is William Buckets, and for the next few minutes, I am going to take you on a journey through the unknown, a journey of discovery.

Our scientists here at Destiny-X Laboratories have been working non-stop to make our latest dream a reality. Behind me is one of the greatest technological advancements known to mankind. Powered by renewable energy, this time capsule is designed to travel through space for perpetuity, carrying the blueprints for a new civilization. Someday, billions of light years away, a society far more advanced than our own will be given the opportunity to reignite the human race, long after our own sun has flickered out. Please join us New Year's Day as we launch the Starland Express . . ."

* * *

The black-tie crowd filed out of the auditorium. Troy decided he couldn't wait another day, let alone another minute. He found Carla amidst a sea of second rate celebrities jockeying for invitations to the after-party. He offered his hand and she accepted unconditionally. The young couple escaped the chaos, driving to the Water Temple, their secret meeting place as kids – one of the few locations in La Fortuna where young lovers could hide from the omnipotent eyes of Billy Buckets.

A pale moon illuminated the temple, its ornate cupola supported by classic Greek columns mounted on a stepped base made of marble. From a distance, the structure resembled the top of a wedding cake, Troy and Carla standing in for the betrothed. The temple was perched at the top of a gentle slope leading down to La Fortuna lake. Carla made a wish and tossed a coin into the dry well, listening as it hit the concrete floor and bounced around, echoing through the tunnels.

Troy smiled, "No water. Does that even count?"

"If you believe, it does."

Carla removed her shoes and took Troy's hand, leading him down a dirt path to the lake. They walked along the cyclone fence until they found an opening and climbed through. The water rippled, lapping at the edge of the shore. Carla took a deep breath and in one fluid motion slipped off her dress, diving into the lake. Troy hesitated, shaking his head in disbelief. "Well, here goes nothing!" He whipped off his shirt, dropped his pants, and plunged into the dark water, resurfacing with a triumphant whoop as he flipped back his long hair, "You're crazy! It's freezing!"

"What are you worried about," Carla teased, "a little shrinkage?"

"Little? I'm probably a eunuch by now."

A loud metallic screech interrupted their laughter. Troy spun around, treading water, "What the hell was that?" He peered into the darkness, further down the shore. "Look, there." Troy pointed to a small jetty where a generator could be heard kicking into gear.

Construction lights switched on, illuminating a large winch reeling a large cylindrical shaped object from the water. A couple of workmen stepped in front of the lights, their silhouettes outlining rifles strapped to their shoulders. A helicopter buzzed overhead.

"C'mon Troy, let's get out of here. This is freaking me out." Carla swam to the shore.

Troy followed, "Yeah, yeah. I'm coming, I'm coming."

They threw on their clothes and hiked back to the car, Troy looking over his shoulder the whole way, determined to make sense of it all.

16

The former darling of the *Jub Jub Club!*, Whitney Fox, sat poolside hosting a weekly poker game at her La Fortuna estate. A group of L.A. rappers lounged around the card table, shielding their eyes from the late afternoon sun. Whitney pushed back her long mane of red hair and reapplied a thick coat of black eyeliner, making her eyes appear more blue than hazel. One of the poker players told her she smelled good, "Is that from one of your perfume lines?" he asked.

"Yup," Whitney smiled as she batted her eyelashes, "It's called Sashay."

The friend cracked up, "Who came up with that one?"

"I don't know, some marketing fruit loop I guess. There's a whole case in my garage if you want some for your girlfriend."

The faint sound of a phone ringing beckoned from inside the house. Whitney perked up, "Deal me out. I'll be back in a minute."

She slipped through a sliding glass door and snatched the phone from a table overflowing with her latest haul of swag. Her accountant's name popped up on the screen – never good news.

Whitney skipped the formalities, "So what now?"

"Well, I hate to be the one to break the news, but It looks like your father has been moving cash from your trust to an off-shore account. From what I can tell he has a mistress and kid in the Cayman Islands. Did you know anything about this?"

Aware of her father's indiscretions, Whitney chose to ignore them. He had been her manager from the beginning, entrusted with a small fortune from her Jub Jub Club days. Only now, the well was running dry. She needed to confront her father soon before things got worse. "Thanks for the heads-up, David. I'll handle the situation from here." She dropped the phone and plopped down in a chair, staring at the stack of promotional gifts lying in a heap on the table. They arrived daily by the truck load, free samples from companies hoping to snag an endorsement from America's top celebutante. Desperate for cash, she had taken to selling the pricier goods on E-Bay, under an assumed name. She rummaged through the swag pile until she came across an item grabbing her attention – a Rubik's Cube. The 3-D puzzle stood out in elegant contrast to the pile of Tiffany and Dolce Gabbana.

* * *

Whitney was eight-years-old when she first set eyes on the popular seventies toy. She had been fishing through a box of her mother's college stuff when she found the colorful plastic cube that fit so nicely in her hand. She obsessed for days, twisting and turning the red, green, blue, and yellow squares until each side of the cube became a single color.

Singing and dancing were not her strong suit as a child actor. Whitney's precocious personality proved to be a far more valuable commodity. However, she did have one unusual talent making her a favorite among the talk show circuit. After delivering a handful of clever one-liners fed by Billy Bucket's writers, Whitney would perform her famous trick, solving the Rubik's Cube in a matter of seconds. Audiences were delighted until the novelty wore thin and they moved on to the next big thing.

Aside from her little carnival act, Whitney possessed another hidden talent – numbers. She was a natural at math. Unfortunately, her education had been uneven at best, and at worst, a complete sham. The producers ran on-set tutoring sessions for Jub Jub Club members. An easy "A" for all guaranteed a smooth production schedule. The studio insisted it was in the best interest of everyone involved.

* * *

Whitney walked outside and set the cube down on the table. She scooted her chair into the shade of the umbrella.

Rapper Dstroy shuffled the cards, gesturing with his chin towards the center of the table. "What is that thing anyway?"

"Don't you know your history boy?" Xcel reached over and picked it up, "It's a Reuben Cube."

"What? It ain't no Reuben cube. It's called a Rubik's Cube dumb-dumb. Give me that thing!" Nero snatched the toy from Xcel's hand. He slouched down in his chair and proceeded to twist the sides back and forth, round and round.

"Damn!" Nero tossed the puzzle back on the table. "It ain't possible. No way!"

"Oh, come on, you big baby!" Whitney teased, "You didn't even try."

"Really? You think you can do it?

"Sure."

"I'll bet you a hundred bucks you can't."

"I'll bet you two hundred I can." She looked

around the table, "Anyone else in?" Dstroy and Xcel slapped down a handful of hundred-dollar bills.

"Five minutes! That's all you get." Xcel warned.

"Five minutes?" Whitney protested.

"Not feeling so smart are we, Einstein?"

Whitney picked up the cube and examined it carefully.

"Uh oh." Nero mocked her in a sing-song voice, "Looks like Da-Whit in trooaubble . . ."

Whitney went at it, furiously twisting and turning the cube in her hands. Less than a minute later she slammed the finished puzzle down on the table, throwing her arms up in victory, "Pay up ladies!"

"Damn!"

"We've been hustled by a chick!"

Whitney punched Excel hard in the shoulder, "Watch your mouth, boy!"

"Hey, everyone shut up!" Nero yelled, "What's that noise?" The friends stopped and listened. A call for help came from inside the house. It was Deadmo.

17

J.J. Powers slouched over his keyboard, exhausted from playing his favorite MMOG all night long. A steady supply of caffeine through the night had dashed any hope of sleep. Candy wrappers, banana peels, and stale coffee cups cluttered his work station. The eighteen-year-old eased back in his chair and felt the stubble on top of his head. J.J.'s chestnut brown skin disguised the fact he spent most days indoors surrounded by computers and toys. Urban vinyl and fantasy action figures populated his work table and shelves. Behind him sat cages and terrariums stacked against a wall. They held the real thing; chameleons, iguanas, rattlers, and more.

J.J. looked up to admire the beasts and warriors

who defined his childhood, scanning the shelves until he came to an empty space where once stood the rarest of fantasy figures, the Ruby Dragella. Toy collectors everywhere coveted the mythical dragon created by Buckets Enterprises. Billy Buckets rewarded J.J. for his work as a Jub Jub Club cast member by giving him the latest limited edition Dragella to roll off the assembly line. Production of the toy ceased years ago, making it impossible to replace. J.J. had not given up "Ruby D." easily, though. He never gave up anything without a fight.

* * *

One day on the set of the *Jub Jub Club!* show, when J.J. was twelve, a young white boy about his age joined the cast of the show. Jordan had been hired to replace his brother, the late Brandon Kraft. He was all smiles and giggles, until the adults turned away. That's when the bullying began. All week long J.J. could smell Jordan's sour breath behind him, teasing and poking him with his finger. J.J. knew fighting on the set could get him fired, jeopardizing his family's meal ticket. But on the last day of the shoot, Jordan whispered a single ugly word into J.J.'s ear. J.J. still can't recall what happened next. Like a car crash, it was over before it began. He found himself covered in blood, but it wasn't his. Jordan laid on the ground, holding his face and screaming. J.J. claimed a light stand had fallen on the new kid.

Unfortunately for J.J., his mother knew better. Right or wrong, her son would pay the price for his violent outburst. When they got home she marched him into his bedroom and ordered her son to pick out one of his treasured Dragellas for disposal. He hesitated, before stepping forward and choosing the Sapphire Dragella. His mother was no fool. She cleared her throat and looked down at J.J, proclaiming, "And the angel of the Lord said unto Abraham, for now I know you fear God, since you have not withheld your only son from me." J.J. lowered his head and walked the Sapphire Dragella back to its perch. Instead, he chose his prized possession to be sacrificed, the Ruby Dragella. But J.J. was no fool either. He snuck out to the garbage can later the same evening and retrieved his only child. He would hide Ruby D. somewhere safe from retribution. He knew just the place.

* * *

J.J.'s phone rang. He checked the number – Whitney again. Probably looking for drugs, J.J. thought. No matter how many times he told her, Whitney seemed incapable of wrapping her head around the fact he never touched the stuff, ever. He answered the phone with a vague sense of dread, "Hey Whit, what's up?"

"Holy crap J.J! You've gotta get over here right now!" She sounded hysterical. J.J wondered who OD'd this time.

"I've got a guy trapped in my bathroom with a rattlesnake blocking the door!"

J.J. thought a moment, "Tell him to get into the

bathtub."

"There's no bathtub. Dammit J.J., get over here now – I need you!"

J.J. looked at his pet rattlesnake resting comfortably in her glass cage, digesting a field mouse, "Well, I guess Dorothy could use a friend. Tell him not to move. I'll be right over."

J.J. grabbed a burlap bag and snake wrangler, jumped into his Bentley, and headed over the hill to Whitney's estate. When he got there, he found everyone huddled in the hallway outside the bathroom door. He recognized Whitney's friends right away. He was not a fan of the three rappers now acting like a bunch of scared little school girls. They always considered themselves way too cool to be associated with a has-been child actor turned nerd herpetologist slash game programmer. Yet, here they stood, a bunch of inked up thugs still bankrolling their dead-end careers with drug money.

J.J. pushed his way past the line and opened the door for a peek. He shook his head in disgust and glared at Whitney, "Really? You actually called me to save this guy's sorry ass?"

Guilt pushed Whitney's shoulders in like a dead weight, "I'm sorry," she whimpered, "I didn't know what else to do. You were the only person I could call."

Unbelievable, J.J. thought. Here he stood, about to help the same low-life who once called him 'Buckwheat', reducing him to a punchline on social media. But J.J. was no fool. He had a plan.

J.J. pushed the door open for everyone to see the badass Deadmo standing on the toilet with his pants around his ankles, his hands covering something the size of a small hamster between his legs. The rattlesnake sat coiled up on a bath mat, within striking distance of Deadmo. J.J. carefully scooped up the reptile with his wrangler, letting the snake dangle precariously close to Deadmo's junk as the rapper sang like a castrato. J.J. had difficulty maneuvering the reptile into the burlap bag. It wasn't easy, wrangling a snake while filming the whole thing on his phone. The internet blew up that night.

18

J.J. drove home from Whitney's house with one eye on the road and the other on the burlap bag squirming around on the passenger seat. Halfway home, a siren blared. He pulled over to the side of the road to let the vehicle pass. Beads of sweat formed on his brow and his hands shook – parked on the exact spot where not long ago, his life changed forever.

* * *

J.J. watched from his rear-view mirror as the La Fortuna security guard strutted up to his car window, "I'll need to see your driver's license and registration, please."

"Yeah, sure." J.J. leaned over to open the glove compartment.

"Slower, please . . ." The guard's fingertips hovering above his holster.

J.J. held out his registration and license.

"Both hands on the steering wheel please." The guard lifted his shades up and squinted for a better look at the registration then back again at J.J.'s driver's license. "This Bentley is really yours, huh?"

The guard leaned down for a closer look at J.J., "Say, are you that rapper guy?"

J.J. flinched, "You're kidding, right?"

The guard stiffened and stepped back from the car, his voice dropping two full octaves, "You need to step out of the car, sir."

J.J. gripped the steering wheel with both hands, "You can't do this! You're not a real cop – you're goddamn Triple-A with a gun." A second guard reached through the passenger side window and tossed something into the glove compartment, pulling it back out and feigning surprise. "So, what do we have here?"

It was Benny Kraft, Jordan's father.

J.J. reached over and slammed the glove compartment door shut, barely missing Kraft's fingers.

"Holy shit!" Kraft screamed. He jerked his gun from its holster, fumbling as it discharged through the open window.

* * *

J.J. came-to, parked in his driveway. He sat for a moment, trying to remember what it was he needed to remember, wondering how he ended up in shorts and flip-flops. It happened sometimes – he would space out and run on auto-pilot for hours. He never told anyone. Didn't want to lose his driver's license. It took over a year and three operations to repair the damage inflicted by the gunshot. J.J. recovered but his career never did. Benny Kraft claimed it was an accident, but J.J. knew better.

J.J. grabbed the burlap bag from the passenger seat and headed into his house, banging around the studio until he found a Plexiglas cylinder about two feet tall. He turned the bag upside down and let the reptile slide into its temporary holding cell. The next few seconds exploded inside J.J.'s head like a super nova. He scrambled to slap the lid back on top of the container, trapping the creature inside. He backed away, holding both hands to his forehead, trying to comprehend what stared back at him. He looked up at the empty space on the bookshelf, between his sapphire and diamond Dragellas, then back at the missing link climbing the side of the plastic cylinder. The frightened creature's chest heaved in unison with J.J.'s. Ribbed wings flinched, a serpentine tail undulated, and red scales shimmered as the tiny dragon released a pint size roar. Ruby D. was back.

19

"No punk kid is going to screw with my empire!" Buckets warned the fourteen-year-old Troy Hatch. He slammed his fist down on the desk sending shock waves through the room. Embers fell like a pile of rocks in the fireplace. They were all alone in the boss's mahogany paneled office. In a dark corner sat Buckets' loyal assistant, a tall well-dressed woman practicing the dead art of short-hand. Who she might be and where she came from had been a source of delectable Hollywood gossip. When Buckets' trusted valet of ten years vanished, the woman appeared at Buckets' side the very next day, as if she had always been there. Rumors swirled, suggesting it was more than sheer coincidence the lady and valet shared the same shoe size.

It was said those who entered Buckets' office left changed forever. How and to what degree depended on Buckets' state of mind. Troy pled his own defense, "It was the body guard's idea!" he insisted, "I'm just a kid. What do I know? I did what they told me to do." Which did not explain the selfie he posted on Instagram. 37.4 million followers were treated to a snap shot of the intoxicated Troy wearing a buffoonish grin with his face squeezed between two female exotic dancers – his second to last act of humiliation, right before he vomited all over them.

Buckets must have been well into his eighties, but he could still make a grown man soil his shorts just by looking at him. He shouted only inches from Troy's face, "You were living out of a van with your parents when I pulled you from the street and put food in your mouth. And this is how you repay me?!"

Three days later, Troy stood on the altar of the *Golden Jubilee* mega-church, flanked on either side by his parents. Even if he could escape, there was nowhere to run, trapped in the middle of Orange County where the bible belt stretched for miles in all directions.

At fourteen, Troy towered over his stepfather. The stubble on his chin required an extra fifteen minutes in makeup before taping. When the *Jub Jub Club!* show went on hiatus, he would abandon the hair brush and let his thick brown hair grow to rock-star length.

Troy shivered at the sight of the freezing water before him, an indoor baptismal the size of a Doughboy pool. The congregation shouted "Hallelujah!" and "Amen!", as a red-faced minister demanded the devil be cast out of Troy's teenage soul. The ritual was his last chance to redeem himself before the almighty Billy Buckets fired his scrawny ass for violating the "moral clause" of his contract.

As he prepared to be born again, Troy pondered what Buckets had said to him that night in his office. Yes, Troy thought, I was poor and desperate just like all the other club members. There were tons of kids from all walks of life in that audition room. Why didn't

Buckets hire one of them? The answer was clear as the water at his feet – control.

Troy stepped into the waist deep pool and met the preacher half-way. The holy man placed one hand on Troy's back and the other on his forehead, plunging him backwards into the cold water. Troy was saved.

* * *

Now nineteen-years-old, Troy's chart topping heavy metal band, *Black Hole*, performed the final sold out show of their world tour at La Fortuna Stadium. He had put a million miles between himself and Billy Buckets since his Jub Jub days. The past few years had been a struggle, but now he was back on top, clad in black leather pants, pacing the arena stage, unleashing raw vocals at maximum volume. Monolithic Jumbo-Trons on either side of the stage played video footage of the Starland Time Capsule launch – Troy's back-handed homage to the *Jub Jub Club!*

Billy Buckets' image loomed large over the stadium

as Troy strutted under the giant screens. Above him played footage from the rocket launch, televised on New Year's Day, when Troy was just sixteen-years-old. The live web stream and telecast garnered over three-hundred million viewers worldwide.

Video showed the young club members lining up along the length of the time capsule, smiling and mugging for the camera. Fourteen-year-old Carla approached first. She held up her contribution for everyone to see, a music box painted with whimsical creatures frolicking in a lush garden. She set the box inside and waved to the television viewers.

Jordan stepped forward. He held up the remote control his brother Brandon had been using the day of the fatal accident, then lowered it into the hull. Buckets bowed his head, placing one hand on Jordan's shoulder – exactly as rehearsed.

Whitney followed close behind, her budding figure on full display in a snug pair of jeans and crop-top. Buckets squirmed with mild discomfort at her performance. She displayed her chosen item with the sweeping gesture of a game show host, winking at the camera as she dropped the Rubik's Cube into the craft.

J.J. stepped forward and presented his Ruby Dragella to the cameras. He smiled and kissed the plastic dragon on the head, placing Ruby inside where she would be safe for eternity.

Harlow stood and watched as a guard gently deposited her prized possession, a Starland snow globe, into the steel shell.

Sixteen-year-old Troy was the last to appear before the cameras. He removed the necklace he was wearing and held it above the open bay doors. At the end of the chain spun a bronze token, his reward for thirty days of sobriety. He struck his best punk rock pose as he lowered it into the capsule. The Starland Park's official press release would later identify the object as a Saint Christopher medal.

Black Hole played to a crescendo as the stadium audience watched the video, counting down in unison, ". . . four . . . three . . . two . . . one . . . lift off!"

The Jumbo-Trons lit up with footage of the rocket

hurtling into the wide blue yonder. The audience roared with approval as pyrotechnics exploded above the stadium. They chanted together, demanding another encore, but Troy was already half way through the stadium service tunnel leading to the arena parking lot.

A gleaming hunk of American muscle waited patiently for its owner to arrive. A Black Mustang Shelby GT500 Super Snake. Troy popped the trunk open and surveyed the contents; backpack, sleeping bag, tent, cooler, and a beat-up cardboard box marked 'Burning Man'. He slammed the trunk closed and slid behind the wheel, executing a clean escape through the stadium gates.

Troy had not told anyone where he was going because he had no idea himself. The concert had been his final obligation before his contract with Buckets Enterprises expired at midnight. The past year had been one last bloodletting before freedom. The road trip would be his declaration of independence. No press, no fans, and no real destination in mind.

Troy shifted into overdrive, flying past a thick

patch of eucalyptus, hugging the edges of the road as the curves narrowed and tightened. He felt the momentum pulling him to the right, then left, and back again. The road became taught, snapping back into a straight line just as an animal darted across his path. He jerked the wheel, but it was too late. The creature flipped over the hood of his car, smashing the windshield. The Shelby spun across the asphalt, landing broadside against a dirt embankment.

Troy shook the glass from his hair. Dazed, he managed to jimmy the door open, lifting himself out of the car. He staggered across the narrow road to a clearing and leaned against a boulder, looking down at his left arm. A couple dozen quills protruded from his shoulder and bicep. He pulled them out, one by one, growing dizzier with each passing second. Something thrashed about in the bushes nearby. He craned his neck, trying to see, but his vision blurred. A warm sensation spilled over him as he lost consciousness, slumping to the ground.

20

The last guest to leave Whitney's house carried away a personal check written for $6,540. In the grand scheme of things, it was a small amount of money to part with for Whitney. But the frequency with which she wrote the checks, on an almost weekly basis, was not sustainable. Gambling seemed like a solid career choice to fall back on, at least when winning. The profits took the sting out of her last perfume line going bust.

Whitney discovered her talent for playing cards a little over a year ago. Soon after, she demonstrated a knack for counting them too. Being underage for just about everything kept her from exploiting her true potential. She needed to earn the respect of Hollywood's high rollers before she could break into the underground world of high stakes poker and hit pay dirt. One big win and she would quit for good, go to college, and make something of her life. No more playing the fake celebrity friend for the highest bidder. No more selfies with old men wearing diapers under tuxedos.

Whitney wandered from table to table collecting empty bottles and dirty paper plates – the day had been an endless stream of cigarettes and diet soda. The sun would be coming up soon, signaling Whitney's bedtime. She retrieved a carton of chocolate ice cream from the refrigerator and headed to an overstuffed chair in the living room, loosening her silk bathrobe before digging into a pile of swag on her dining room table where the Rubik's cube lay within reach. She couldn't resist. Less than fifty seconds later she solved the puzzle. A slight improvement over her performance earlier in the day.

Whitney's phone dinged like a dinner bell. A chain of text messages popped up on her phone screen, all from Nero. *"Got some players here . . . willing to bet 10k their guy can kick your Rubik's cube ass . . . easy $$ . . . r u down?"*

"Hell yeah!" Whitney wrote, *"Game on!"* She dropped back into her chair to ponder the future. This could be it, she thought, no more small time. Nothing but rainbows and unicorns dead ahead. She stared at the cube on the table. The toy appeared to pulsate and change shape. She rubbed her eyes and blinked. The vibration became more extreme, the puzzle now floating above the table top. A blue light escaped from between the seams, pushing apart the individual plastic cubes. The more she focused on the light, the greater the clarity. Time and space no longer impeded a world unbound by earthly tenants. Fear and doubt receded from Whitney's mind as she waded through the knowledge of a thousand lifetimes. Perfection hung in the air, tangible and within her grasp. Then just like that, a cold hard fear came boomeranging back a hundredfold, shattering the cosmic seduction. She pulled herself free from the trance and opened her eyes

as the cube contracted, falling to the table.

Whitney gasped for air and swallowed. A foul metallic taste filled her nostrils as a wave of nausea pushed her towards the bathroom. A fountain of blue liquid shot out of her mouth. She leaned over the sink and washed away the strings of saliva clinging to her chin. Something loose rolled around on her tongue. She spat it out and looked down at her hand for confirmation. It was a diamond ring. A two and a half karat rock commemorating her sweet sixteen. She rinsed it off and placed it back on her index finger, staggering down the hall to her bedroom.

She laid on her bed, cradling her midsection with both arms. The events of the evening remained scattered in her mind. Tomorrow she would piece them back together, constructing a perfectly acceptable explanation.

21

Troy lifted himself off the ground, swaying in the cold morning air as he tried to recollect the events leading to his disheveled state. He could now see the old fire road in the light of day. A forbidden but convenient short cut he had taken to reach the main highway. He slid down an incline to reach the road kill, nudging its belly with a stick. Rigor mortis had set in. He examined the body, covered in quills with no discernable eyes, mouth, or tail, giving the creature the appearance of an enormous pine cone laying on its side. The animal measured over five feet in length with powerful hind legs tucked up against its abdomen. The feet resembled an ostrich's, each with two giant toes, forming a lethal set of claws. Whatever it was, it was going home with him – if not for science, then for sheer freak show value. He threw his camping gear into the back seat, spreading out a tarp and loading the dead animal into the trunk of his car. He peeled back the shattered front windshield just enough to see the road and headed home with an amazing story.

* * *

Troy laid the dead animal on the cement floor of his garage. At second glance, he decided the thing looked more like a cross between a giant mole and a porcupine. He called the Los Angeles County Department of Animal Control to report his incredible find. They too found his story truly unbelievable, explaining they had neither the budget nor the patience for childish pranks. He called the only veterinarian in La Fortuna, but her office was closed on Sundays. He went online but found nothing even remotely resembling what lay in a heap on his garage floor.

A handful of hunting trips with his stepfather taught Troy it wouldn't be long before the carcass began to smell. He would have to gut the animal if he wanted to preserve the remains. That was the first thing he read when he googled "How to dress a deer." He wouldn't skin the animal, just remove the organs to inhibit decay, and store the remainder in his garage freezer for safe keeping.

Troy hung the beast upside down from a rafter in the garage and proceeded to slice it open from pelvis to sternum. The contents of the stomach spilled out onto the floor, barely missing his shoes. He grabbed a dust pan, scooping up the gelatinous mess when something caught his eye. He grabbed a screw driver and fished the object out of the foul-smelling muck, washing it off in the utility sink. A slightly tarnished metal chain glimmered under the overhead light. He held up the necklace. A bronze token slowly turned at the end of the chain. He dropped the keepsake into a nearby coffee can and proceeded to finish the job.

A warm shower did little to relieve the anxiety of

the last twenty-four hours. Barefoot and shirtless, Troy plopped down on his living room couch and dried his hair with a towel. Something sharp pricked his finger. He pulled the errant quill from his tangled hair and held it between his fingers, recalling the sense of euphoria he experienced just before losing consciousness in the woods. He snapped the quill in two and watched as a drop of thick amber liquid formed at the tip. He tasted it with his tongue. The effect was like a sunburst, an exploding cloud of pure nirvana. He drifted higher and higher, until he was looking down at an earthly existence populated by lost souls ignorant of the infinite. A simmering presence filled the room as something cold touched his chest. The bronze token now dangled from his neck.

"This will protect you." A woman's voice whispered.

"From what?" Troy asked.

"From you."

22

Ruby hadn't eaten a thing since moving into her new home. J.J. pegged her for a carnivore, judging from the sharp talons and teeth, but when offered a field mouse, she ignored it. He tried placing a variety of foliage in her cage but she barely touched the fresh greens. Maybe she only eats sporadically, like a snake, he thought. Regardless, Ruby continued to surprise J.J. with a prolific output of poop. He scooped up her waste along with wood shavings and dumped the contents on to a compost pile next to the garage. Doing so, he noticed a plant protruding from a pile of Ruby's droppings, discarded the day before. He bent down for a closer look, pushing away dead leaves surrounding the base of the stalk. Seeds the size of black peppercorns lay scattered about, no doubt a part of Ruby's diet before she had arrived. J.J. gathered up the seedlings and spent the rest of the day planting them in pots. The plants in the shade appeared far more robust than those shriveling in the sun, so he decided to move the containers inside the house, hoping they would fare better. He added a little fertilizer for good measure.

The plants' rate of growth stunned J.J., four feet in only three days with buds forming at the top. He let Ruby out of her cage and set her down next to the pots. Much to his relief, Ruby munched on the leaves, whittling the stalks down to half their height. J.J.'s instincts proved right, his experiment a success. He got to work creating a hydroponic garden. By the end of the weekend, his basement resembled a forest. The plants almost touching the ceiling. Ruby sprouted up too, almost three feet tall with a six-foot wing span, outgrowing the confines of the garage. J.J. got to work transforming his spacious attic into a Dragella roost, equipped with a skylight for ventilation. When he introduced Ruby to her new home, she spread her wings and flew up to the rafters, clearly pleased with the new digs. J.J. knew he couldn't keep her inside forever, but day time excursions remained out of the question. One glimpse of his Dragella and the world would be at his door. He decided evening forays into the nearby hills would work fine.

* * *

The sun set as J.J. prepared to take Ruby into the nearby wilderness to stretch her wings. He attached a GPS tracker to her ankle and brought along a bag of buds from the plants in the basement. They would come in handy if he needed to coax her back into the car.

Ruby enjoyed the ride into the hills, pushing her snout through a crack in the window and sniffing the fresh air. J.J. turned off the asphalt road and on to a dirt fire lane. The tall dry grass appeared silver in the moonlight. Magnificent oak trees dotted the rolling hills. J.J. walked ruby a short distance from the car and removed the dog leash. She hopped in a circle around her master, afraid to venture away. J.J. decided a higher vantage point might encourage lift off. He corralled her on to the roof of his car, the bike rack serving as a perch. The plan worked beautifully. Ruby took off into the night. J.J. stood in awe as he watched the silhouette of his childhood friend soar through the deep purple sky, circling overhead as she called into the night.

23

Nero stood in the background behind a clump of spectators who had come to watch the show. The venue was an abandoned slaughterhouse on the edge of town, still haunted by the smell of pig's blood soaked into the floorboards. Whitney had demanded all phones and recording devices be collected at the door, one of her many conditions for participating in the illicit affair. She broke through the crowd and approached the table in the center of the room. A horde of sweaty men bathed in fluorescent light showered her with whistles and catcalls, all betting on her to fail. She held up her purse, indicating she was good for the thirty grand and sat down. Her opponent held court at the opposite end of the table, his face obscured by a baseball cap and hoodie. The challengers had found him on YouTube where he claimed to be a world champion 'cuber'. Whitney wasn't impressed, she just wanted to collect her money and get the hell out of there.

The referee for the evening stepped forward and inspected each of the cubes, twisting and turning them until satisfied they had been sufficiently scrambled. He set them down in front of their respective owners. The crowd buzzed with anticipation, pushing the noise level higher. The referee held an air horn above his head and shouted instructions, "Both hands face down on the table!" The players obliged. "Alright, on your mark, get set, GO!!" He sounded the horn and the race began.

Whitney's fingers fumbled over the surface of the cube. The blood pumping past her ear drums drowned out the screaming crowd. Twenty-nine seconds later Whitney solved the puzzle, but success came too late. Her opponent slammed his finished cube down on the table first. The spectators high-fived each other. A man shaped like an action figure stepped forward and nodded to Whitney – time to pay up. She opened her purse, lingering over the bag. The man lost his patience, snatching it out of her hand and looking inside. His displeasure registered clear across the room.

Whitney spotted Nero, backing away towards the exit. Her voice wavered, "I, um . . . I must have grabbed the wrong purse on the way out . . ."

Two large men grabbed Nero and dragged him over to Whitney. They held his arms behind his back and pushed his face down on the table.

"No, no, no . . ." Whitney pleaded, "It's ok, really . . ." She pulled a wallet from her bag. "Look, I have it! Right here . . ." she held up a credit card. "You take Visa, right?"

"Break his arm!" One of the men yelled.

"Oh, god no!" Nero screamed, "Please, please no!!"

Then it happened, and not a minute too soon. Whitney's cube burst open, a brilliant light filling the room and paralyzing the men. The cube hovered above the table, an intense ball of energy, turning in the air. Whitney wasted no time, grabbing the cash off the table and stuffing her purse. She shook Nero, still bent over with his face smashed into the table. "Get up, get up!" Whitney cried. She pushed away the two thugs, standing with their arms hanging at their sides like a couple of rag dolls. Nero lifted his head off the table and opened his eyes, immediately hypnotized by the light. Whitney slapped him hard in the face, "Nero! Wake-up! Wake-up!" He blinked. She grabbed his chin and turned him away from the cube. "Nero, don't look at the light, whatever you do, don't look at the light!" She pulled him towards the exit, "Oh no, wait, wait!" She spun around and swung her purse at the floating cube. It collapsed into its original size, falling to the floor. She scooped it up and turned towards Nero, frozen in place again. She slapped him even harder this time, pushing him outside, "I said don't look at the light you fricking idiot!"

Nero stumbled across the parking lot, looking around, "Where are we?"

"Never mind, get in the car." Whitney shoved Nero in and slammed the door shut.

The tires squealed as they turned onto the road, the warehouse shrinking in the rear-view mirror at seventy miles an hour. Whitney was ecstatic, "We did it, we did it!"

"Did what?" Nero rubbed his jaw.

Whitney dumped the contents of her purse on to Nero's lap – stacks of hundred-dollar bills spilled out.

"What the hell Whitney! Did you steal this? They're gonna kill us!"

"Relax! No one is gonna kill anyone."

What are you talking about?"

"No one in that room is going to remember a thing. As far as they know, we never showed up."

"How do you know that?"

"Do you remember what you did last Thursday night?"

"What? No, why?"

"Or Wednesday?"

"I . . . I don't know."

"Monday Night?"

"Ok, ok! What the hell is going on?"

"We've been running the same scam all week. We've made $40,000.00 so far!"

"Shut up!" Nero blurted. "Just shut up. You're crazy!"

Whitney pulled into the parking lot of a Seven-Eleven. "Here." She picked up her phone and played back video. "See, there you are. Remember that? Or how about that? That was the first night. I tried to tell you then, but you were totally out of it . . . and you see that there in the background? That's a big pile of cash . . . and it's all ours!"

It was all sinking in for Nero, "Where's the money now?" he asked.

"Ah . . ." Whitney laughed, "Now you believe me!"

24

Troy pulled his face away from the couch cushions and sat up. The house was dark and cold. He walked to a bar in the corner of the room and guzzled water from the faucet, dousing the fire in his throat. Something crackled under his feet. He tapped the dimmer switch and squinted, looking down. Spread across the floor and coffee table laid dozens of quills. Each one cracked open and empty. He picked up his phone and turned it on, too many messages to count – four days had passed. He sunk into an overstuffed leather chair and pulled his knees up to his chest. He knew all too well what was coming next. Any last remnants of euphoria had been smothered by a sinister concoction of dread and self-loathing. He sat in silence as the worst day of his life played back in his head.

* * *

The girl had to be at least eighteen-years-old to work at Starland Amusement Park. That's where they met, at a photo shoot in front of Bandersnatch Adventure. One of the security guards told Troy to check out the park's mascot Jub Jub when she took off her head. He did – she was beautiful, with long dark shiny hair and golden skin. Small enough to fit into the costume but with a personality big enough to fill the park. To this day, Troy still cannot remember her name – back then he was pretty much high all the time.

When the iron fist of Billy Buckets was finally laid to rest, the club members lost their way – and their minds, at least temporarily. The only discipline they had ever known vanished overnight. Their parents were now their employees, and their fans the ultimate enablers. The teenage stars ran wild through the streets of La

Fortuna as security looked the other way.

One night, Troy threw a party with over two hundred guests. They filled the first floor of his house, spilling out into the pool area. Pop stars, actors, socialites, and wannabes – just another Saturday night in La Fortuna. The bouncer at the front door texted Troy, "*Frankie's here.*"

Troy stood on his toes to see over the packed crowd, but it wasn't necessary – Frankie Wilson towered over everyone. Once a talented athlete with a promising future in pro football, a series of missteps prematurely ended his dream. Now he hung out in his apartment making music all day and selling drugs at night.

Jordan poked Troy, "Dude! Dude! Look who Frankie's with." It was Whitney Fox, trailing close behind.

Troy's jaw tightened. Two months had passed since the night he broke up with Whitney. She had gotten drunk at a club and punched a girl in the face for trying to take a selfie with him. Rumors of mental illness and drug abuse followed, branding Whitney the "crazy ex-girlfriend" – which made her even crazier. Whitney's management shut down her social media accounts and committed her to a seventy-two hour psychiatric evaluation.

Troy turned to Jordan and slipped a roll of hundreds into his hand, "Would you mind doing the honors. I don't want to get anywhere near her." Jordan agreed, meeting up with Frankie in the middle of the dance floor to close the deal.

Troy's phone buzzed with a new message from the bouncer, "*She's here.*" He made his way to the front door and took the young girl's hand. Jub Jub never looked so good. Her smile lit up the room, thrilled to be in the presence of so many stars. A part-time employee and full-time student, she was still new to the ways of young Hollywood.

Whitney glared at the happy couple from the opposite side of the room. She stood perfectly still, holding a drink that rarely left her lips. When Troy's date slipped away to use the restroom, Whitney followed and stood in line with her, striking up a conversation. When the girl's turn came to use the bathroom, Whitney kindly offered to hold her drink.

A slew of D.J.s kept the party humming into the early morning hours, long after everyone had left. When Troy opened his eyes, he found himself laying on top of his bed fully clothed. He got up and walked to the bathroom, pausing at the doorway to comprehend what lay on the floor. It was the girl, her eyes half open, vomit trailing from her mouth. She was cold to the touch. Troy must have yelled because someone came running up the stairs. It was Frankie, and for the right price, he knew exactly what to do.

* * *

Troy's joints ached, his t-shirt drenched in cold sweat. He could hardly hold a single thought for more than a few seconds without being consumed by a need to satiate his new addiction. He went to the garage, pacing back and forth in front of the freezer – reaching for the handle, then pulling back again. The tug-of-war went on and on until he abruptly cursed and yanked the door open. The animal's hide had been picked clean. He rushed back to the living room and fell on all fours, desperately searching for stray quills. A finely manicured hand reached down and lifted Troy's chin until he was looking into a pair of emerald green eyes. It was the lady. She had a message.

25

J.J. woke up on his couch, holding a pillow over his head to drown out the sound of Ruby hopping around the attic, squawking and scratching the floor. She was hungry. J.J. ran outside to fetch a bag of plant buds from his car, returning empty handed with pieces of broken glass stuck to the bottom of his shoes. He checked the security footage. Sure enough, there they were – Deadmo's entourage busting the car window and pillaging the contents of his Bentley, no doubt in retaliation for the video J.J. had posted online.

The phone rang. J.J. hustled down the hall, knocking his head on low hanging vines as he turned and entered the studio. The plant, now enormous, climbed along the walls and ceiling. At least a dozen football shaped pods dangled overhead. He grabbed the phone, answering before it went to voicemail.

"Yeah, this is J.J."

"Que pasa, brother?" It was Deadmo.

J.J. was furious, "You've got a lot of nerve sending your guys over here to break into my car! I caught the whole thing on my security camera, asshole!"

"Hey man, really sorry about that. No worries, I'll pay for the damage . . . just tell me where you got the stuff."

"What stuff?!"

"That crazy weed, man! Where did you get it?

"What the hell are you talking about?"

"That weed they found in your car, man. It's totally off the hook. Xcel is seeing laser cats and shit. Where can I get some more?"

It suddenly occurred to J.J. what Deadmo was talking about. The idiots had smoked Ruby's plants. "That's not weed you moron! It's food for my pet!"

"Whatever it is, it's dope man. C'mon, how much you want?"

"It's not for sale! Don't call me again and stay the hell away from my house." J.J. slammed the phone down on his desk and sank back into his chair. Ruby sensed J.J.'s frustration, nuzzling her wet nose against his neck. He smiled, swiveling his chair around to reciprocate – but it wasn't Ruby. A drooling pod bobbed up and down, inches from his face, splitting open to reveal a lethal set of razor sharp teeth. JJ. dove to the ground and scrambled across the tile floor. Half a dozen pods came to life, snapping at his feet. He grabbed a small metal garbage can from under his desk and shielded himself against the pods as they took turns striking him in a whipsaw motion, his odds of escape shrinking dramatically. Suddenly, the studio door burst open and Ruby charged in, decapitating the pods with lethal claws and gnashing teeth, ripping the green monster to shreds. She gnawed at the remains until satisfied the plant was dead.

J.J. stumbled into the living room, still gasping for air, his mind careening towards a horrible realization – the basement! He bolted for the garage, diving through

179

stacks of saws and hammers until he found the gardener's machete. He gripped the handle tight and practiced slicing the air. "Good enough." He charged down the hall calling for backup, "C'mon Ruby! Let's go, girl!"

J.J. kicked open the basement door and descended the dark staircase. Ruby stopped at the top of the landing unable to maneuver the steps, leaving J.J. on his own. He turned on the light switch, preparing to swing away but the room was completely empty. No plants, no pots, no lights. Even the fertilizer and extension cords were gone, "Oh, no . . . Deadmo!" He ran upstairs and texted the rapper. No answer. J.J. hated the guy, but not enough to see him get eaten alive. He grabbed the machete and headed out.

26

The gates to Deadmo's villa were swung wide open. J.J. parked his car on the side of the road behind a clump of trees and sat for a moment listening. No music playing, no pit bulls barking, not a sound. He crept up the driveway to the motor court, filled with BMWs, Mercedes, and Hummers, all tricked out with chrome detailing and titanium rims. He used the machete to push open the front door of the house, flipping on the main light switch with his elbow. The living room came to life with strobe lights and thumping base. Deadly vines smothered the walls. J.J. stiffened, ready to swing, but the man-eating pods didn't move. Instead, they hung low to the ground, their appetite satiated. Lazy-Boys and lamp shades had been knocked over, splattered with fresh blood. The plants clearly preferred the more delicate flesh of human organs, leaving heads and limbs scattered about the room. A pair of disembodied legs sat on the couch, a bong squeezed between bloody thighs – poised for another hit.

J.J. dropped the machete and stumbled outside, vomiting until his stomach was empty, then retching some more. He leaned against a fence and drank from a garden hose, his body vibrating, his mind flashing on the gruesome carnage inside. No way could he risk the plants spreading through La Fortuna. He unstrapped a five gallon can of gas from the back of a Hummer, then marched into the house, splashing gasoline around the living room. He tossed a book of lit matches on to the soaked carpet and waited in his car with the engine idling, until the flames had fully engulfed the house.

27

Agent Gummer pulled a crumpled Kleenex from his coat pocket and covered his nose. "For crissakes! You'd think I'd be used to the smell by now!"

Gummer's young assistant came scrambling up the hill with a container of Vick's VapoRub.

"Forget it." The agent growled, "Too late." He stood where the driveway met the house, a few feet from a pile of smoldering embers and flesh, "Where's forensics? Harris!" Gummer's voice bounced around the canyon below, "What've you got?"

"Probably five males, in their twenties . . . "

"Probably?"

"Well, five heads anyway. We're still searching for the rest."

"Geesus! What the hell happened here?"

"Can't say for sure yet, but it looks like the bodies were dismembered first, then burned."

"H-o-l-y crap!"

Harris held up a machete already bagged and tagged, "I found this, but I don't think it's the murder weapon. No blood on it. It looks like the victims were ripped apart by a wild animal of some kind. A lot of crushed bone and teeth marks. Maybe a mountain lion."

"Did it burn down the house too?" Gummer spit on the ground. "I'm never gonna get this taste out of my mouth."

Another one of Gummer's assistants approached the group, looking down at an iPad, "Definitely arson sir. Fire started in the living room. I found a bucket and hose at the bottom of the stairwell. Looks like he had an indoor pot farm. Hydroponics equipment in the basement."

"He?"

"Yeah, the owner of the residence. Frankie Wilson, A.K.A. Deadmo. Made it big a few years ago, had a

186

couple of hits, then kind of disappeared from the scene."

"How do you know all that?"

"Fan, sir."

Gummer rolled his eyes, "What about the others?"

The assistant motioned towards the burned-out SUVs, "We checked the plates. Most of the vehicles were leased to the victims. All males in their twenties. All locals. I asked the office to do a preliminary check on social media. It appears they all knew each other, members of Deadmo's entourage.

"So, what do you think sir?" the assistant asked.

"Hell if I know." Gummer mumbled. "Murder by Mountain Lion? Keep the details out of the press until we know more. I don't want the good people of La Fortuna freaking out on us . . . and alert the park service in case there's anything out there.

Gummer studied the ground for a moment, "Harris, what's the status on the Jane Doe we found in Benet's bathroom?"

"We received the DNA results. It's an exact match, sir."

"Unbelievable. Don't say a damn word to anybody. You understand?

"Yes sir."

"What about the new guy, the driver, do we have him in place?"

"Yes, sir."

Gummer looked down at the valley below, "One hell of a view. No wonder these Hollywood assholes live up here." He rubbed the back of his neck and looked up, "What's that damn noise?"

"Drone sir. Paparazzi can't get past the gates so they send in drones."

"Murphy!" Gummer yelled to the agent standing guard. "You duck hunt?" He shaped his thumb and forefinger into a gun and pointed at the drone.

"Yes, sir!" The agent lifted his shotgun and blasted the offending target out of the sky, "Like fish in a barrel sir!"

28

The sound of a gunshot sent Troy diving to the ground and ducking behind a tree. He heard voices coming from the ridge above and looked up. Men in uniform milled about, inspecting the grounds of Deadmo's estate. He scrambled another twenty yards to a tree stump marking the spot and dug with his bare hands, hitting the top of a plastic storage tub. He pulled the cover off, revealing a cache of guns and ammo leftover from Deadmo's drug dealing days. He stuffed a duffle bag with all the guns he could carry and covered his tracks, hiking back to his car half a mile away.

Troy drove to the site where he had crashed his car days before. He parked his Shelby off the fire road, in the brush, covering the car with a dark green tarp and tree branches. The effect of the quills' toxin was wearing off. His hands shook. He tried to calm himself with deep breaths, but that only made him hyper-ventilate. He slung the duffle bag over his shoulder, trudging along the dry creek bed, scanning the side of the canyon wall. There it was, exactly where the lady said it would be. He cleared away the dry brush covering the rusted metal door and pried it open. Dark and dank, the interior resembled a medieval dungeon. Troy moved his hand up and down on both sides of the doorway until he found the light switch, continuing down a spiral metal stairwell to a thirty by thirty foot concrete bunker almost two stories high. A mass of interweaving metal pipes filled the room, crisscrossing above and lining the walls. Straight ahead was a large valve wheel with an assortment of pressure gages attached. Troy suddenly realized where he was, in the pump room of La Fortuna's waterways. He heard something and cocked his head to listen. It sounded like an animal's cry. Not quite a dog, higher pitched, like a hawk or owl. It came from behind a cluster of pipes in the far corner of the room. He reached the rear wall where he found a large sliding steel door and gripped the handle with both hands, pulling with all his might. The two-inch thick door scraped along rusty tracks as it slid open.

A whole new smell came drifting out from the other side, along with a cacophony of sounds. His mind flooded with memories of visiting the city zoo as a kid. The smell of wet hay mixed with the sour stench of animal dung. His eyes adjusted to the dim glow of phosphorescence clinging to the walls. He was no longer standing on a concrete floor, but surrounded by a dirt tunnel about twelve feet in diameter. Cubby holes of varying sizes had been dug into both sides of the tunnel, some large enough to accommodate a grown man, all of them teeming with life. He could only make out random features; a striped tentacle, a flickering tongue, iridescent scales glowing in the dark. There were no bars or visible barriers holding them back, yet they remained in their enclosures, undisturbed by Troy's presence. He walked past one exotic creature after another. Some appeared to float or hover, weaving and bobbing in place, while others slithered through the air like eels traversing ocean waters. He finally found what the lady had promised him – the creature appeared to be sound asleep. Troy took off his jacket and wrapped it around the end of his gun, reaching into the den and nudging the animal's hind quarters. He pulled it back out and plucked the quills from his jacket, cracking them in half and sucking out the intoxicating elixir, quelling the agony of withdrawal. He leaned against the dirt wall and thought about what the lady had said, "You will save them all, and in doing so, save yourself."

"Hello? Is anybody down there?" A man's voice echoed through the cave from the pump room above. Troy tightened his grip on the AK-47 he cradled in his arms.

"Is anybody in here? This is the Park Ranger speaking. You are in a restricted area. You need to leave the premises, immediately!"

Troy could hear the man's boots scraping along the concrete floor. He hoped the ranger wouldn't notice the open metal door behind the tangle of pipes. He prayed the man would go away. He didn't want to kill anybody, not if he didn't have to. "Not everyone will make it." the lady had told him, "Sacrifices will be made and heroes buried."

29

Carla paced around the foyer, waiting for the driver to arrive. She checked her phone one last time, hoping to find a message from Troy – something to explain his absence for the last week. Even his bandmates thought it strange, not showing up for his own wrap party, taking off on a trip to god knows where. Black Hole's manager called every police station and hospital within fifty miles. Thankfully, they had nothing to report.

Carla's stylist decided his client's look for the day's event should be one of grace and elegance. The kind of tailored ensemble one would wear to a polo match, or tea with the Queen. Civic events rarely offered photo ops worthy of teen stars on the brink of a comeback, but Carla decided to make an exception for the Mayor's water conservation project. Think global, act local. It was this or accompany Jordan to the book signing of his latest memoir, his third in as many years. Jordan's literary agent was elated when he heard Carla would not be joining them. He always felt her presence was a downer for "Krafties", young female fans who harbored the fantasy of one day becoming Mrs. Jordan Kraft. Carla never new whether to laugh or cry when she saw them.

Lupita came down the stairs, "Miss Carla, you look wonderful!"

"Oh, thank you."

"Do you need these?" Lupita held up one of Carla's pill containers. Carla hesitated, slightly embarrassed, "I suppose so, thanks." Her phone buzzed. The driver had arrived.

Lupita opened the front door, "You have nice time now Miss Carla, ok?"

"Always do!" Carla rolled her eyes for the housekeeper who giggled as she waved goodbye.

The new driver stood at attention in front of a

spotless white Land Rover. He was young, handsome, and impeccably dressed in a suit and tie. With his dark hair, square build, and movie star looks he could have been Carla's date for the evening and no one would have blinked.

Carla smiled, "It's Judah, Right?"

"Yes, ma'am."

"So, how are things, Judah?"

"Very good Miss Shane, and you?"

"I'll let you know when the day is over."

Judah leaned down to open the passenger door for Carla, his jacket flapping open to reveal a holstered gun – a startling reminder that he was not just her driver, but bodyguard too. A former member of the Israeli Special Forces, Judah was both charming and lethal. He was a new addition to a rotating staff of service people. Carla knew she was in good hands but it did little to soothe her nerves when it came to fanatics and stalkers.

* * *

When she was thirteen, Carla's new-found celebrity had drawn an unseemly type of fan – crazies obsessed with making that allusive connection at any cost. One night, while Dina was up late organizing Carla's weekly schedule, she heard a loud thump upstairs. She assumed it was her husband whose nightly routine of self-medicating usually ended with him passing out in one of the guest bedrooms. Two loud pops followed, raising the hairs on the back of her neck. She rushed upstairs to find her husband laying in a pool of blood under an open window – the anonymous intruder long gone.

Carla remembered the sound of a Vienna Waltz filling her room that night, and her mother appearing at her bedside, smoothing her hair and whispering, "Everything is going to be okay now." Over time Carla would manage to push the details of that evening into the distance, until there was very little left to recall.

* * *

Carla swayed from side to side as the Rover snaked through the hills. She glanced at her phone for messages and cursed. The battery was dead. Judah pulled to the curb and hopped out, opening the door for Carla. She avoided stepping on the wet grass as she waded into a crowd of more than a hundred people. A red velvet rope draped across construction barriers kept the press at bay. She surveyed the crowd. The *Real Housewives of La Fortuna* were on parade, shimmering in Versace. Despite a slight breeze, their hair remained fused together with an abundance of product. The women kept busy taking selfies, immortalizing their frozen foreheads for mass consumption.

Carla stood on a tiny island of flagstone, poised with a glass of fake champagne in her hand. She feigned a modicum of anticipation as she gazed up at a row of twenty dump trucks parked at the edge of the lake, overflowing with 96 million plastic shade balls. They were the city's latest attempt to slow evaporation and save water during a record-breaking drought, now in its third year.

Honorary Mayor and local weatherman, Perris Raines, stepped up to the microphone, "Welcome one and all," he announced, "to this exciting and historic event. On behalf of the citizens of La Fortuna I would like to thank all the donors who made this wonderful gift possible. And now, without further ado . . ." Raines gave the signal and twenty truck drivers lifted the last of their payloads into the sky as the black spheres, each the size of a bowling ball, rolled down the clay embankment and into the water. Floating side by side, they looked like caviar spread across a cracker the size of five football fields. The guests applauded and cameras flashed. Carla's job was done – it was time to go. She made her way to the exit, chin up, smiling like a beauty queen. A familiar voice rose from the crowd, laughing and conversing. She turned. There stood Jenna Stanfield, alive and well, holding court among La Fortuna's elite. Carla became unsteady, perspiring under her couture – her cone of vision shrinking to the size of a keyhole. It all came flooding back like a lucid dream. If not Jenna, then who? She righted herself and shook it off, she had to – the alternative was unthinkable.

"Oh, Carla!" Jenna called out, "So sorry to hear about Troy. I'm sure he'll be fine. Give him my best, would you?" She seemed to enjoy delivering the mysterious news. Carla maintained her composure, refusing to make eye contact, weaving towards the valet stand.

Judah pulled up in the Land Rover, pushing the valet aside to open the door for Carla. She took a seat in the back, gulping down a bottle of Evian water along with a couple of pills she found at the bottom of her purse. She plugged her phone into a charger between the seats. It dinged over and over with a flurry of messages,

"AGAIN???"

"Wasn't he a #JubJubkid?"

"Stupid f**king show!"

"Hopes and prayers for Troy."

Carla clicked on a fresh TMZ video. There sat Troy, his face distorted by a laptop camera. "I want to apologize for letting everyone down. It's just a bump in the road. I'm feeling much better now." Troy grasped the bronze token hanging from his neck and held it up to the camera, "See, they even gave me back my lucky charm. I'm bullet proof now."

The last few days flashed through Carla's mind. Troy had been stone cold sober the last time she saw him. None of it made sense. Her phone vibrated again.

"Carla, honey . . . Its Dina. I want you to listen, and listen carefully. This is not what you need right now, especially after you just went through this sort of thing yourself . . ."

"This sort of thing?"

"You know what I mean. I don't need to tell you how much is riding on this new show. Expectations are very high darling. I know you're under a lot of pressure and . . ."

"Where is he?"

"Carla, you need to step back and take a deep breath. Let this Troy thing play itself out."

"Tell me where he is!"

"He's in good hands."

"Where?"

"With Dr. Doug, but . . ."

Carla hung up. "Judah, pull over!"

"Is everything OK, ma'am?"

"Just pull over . . . there, at that gas station!"

Judah turned into the driveway and came to a full stop. He jumped out to open the door for Carla, but she was already standing on the pavement, gathering her things off the back seat. "Judah, I own this thing, right?"

"The car? Well, it's leased by your company if that's what you mean."

"Good." She held out her hand, "Give me the keys."

"Uh . . . well, they're in the ignition but . . ."

Carla jumped into the SUV and stepped on the gas, turning the steering wheel hard as she swung the car around. Judah leapt out of the way, waving his hands in the air and shouting, "Dina isn't going to like this!" The roar of the engine drowned out his protest as Carla accelerated, heading off for New Horizons, Dr. Doug's mothership.

30

"I'm afraid I don't see your name anywhere on the manifest, ma'am."

Carla lowered her sunglasses and took a gamble. Considering this was Los Angeles, her odds were pretty good. "You're an actor, aren't you?"

"Yeah, that's right. How did you know?" He pointed to his security badge. "This is just my day job. Ever seen *Galactica Force*?"

"Gee, no. I'm sorry."

"*Black Talons*? I played a ninja in that one."

"Well, I'm sure you were very good. I can always tell. Why don't you give me your name and number? I'll pass it along to my agent." Carla tapped and swiped her phone.

The guard couldn't believe his luck – stumbling over the spelling of his own name.

"Got it." Carla winked. "Now, the gate?"

"Oh, yeah . . . right." He raised the metal arm and playfully saluted as she drove past. The car snaked up a brick driveway lined with rose bushes. The manicured hospital grounds exuded an ambiance more resort than rehab. She parked next to a red curb in front of the main office building and marched through the automatic sliding doors. The hallway walls displayed inspirational posters featuring Dr. Doug promoting good health and clean living. "Fight like a Fan!", one read, cheering on his celebrity clientele.

Carla approached the front desk and hit her mark, "I'm here to see Troy Hatch." She glanced at her watch adding a sense of urgency to her performance, "He's expecting me."

The receptionist was unimpressed. "I'm sorry, but there is no one here by that name."

Carla cleared her throat, "Maybe he's registered under a different name. I'm his girlfriend . . . " Carla liked the sound of that.

"Even if he was here, which he's not, it's past visiting hours."

"Well, I guess I'll have to come back later."

"Yes, you do that." The nurse didn't bother looking up from her computer.

Carla exited the building and changed course, entering an adjacent facility through an unmarked door. She strolled down a hallway with stained acoustic tiles and peeling paint – a stark contrast from the slick marble floors of the main building. Each room had an oversized metal door with an eight-inch square of safety glass at eye level. She peered through the windows as she walked, catching glimpses of errant office furniture and beat-up bed pans. One of the doors had been left ajar, offering a clear view of the interior. A pink quilt covered a hospital bed, topped with an assortment of stuffed animals. There were bars on the windows. She leaned in for a better look. Jub-Jub's head sat in a corner, the fur discolored and nose scuffed, still wearing that dopey grin – his bottom half nowhere to be found.

The sound of someone pushing a cart through the hall was Carla's cue to keep moving. She turned a corner and passed through double doors leading to another wing of the building. A reception area sat vacant, lit from above by a single panel of fluorescent lights. She stepped behind the reception desk and searched for a roster, manifest, anything that could tell her where Troy might be. A bank of video monitors lit up the counter top. One of the screens captured a young girl pacing back and forth. The video had no sound but Carla could see the girl was under duress, waving her hands and yelling into a mirror, clawing at her reflection. Carla moved closer and squinted. The girl wore the bottom half of the Jub-Jub costume.

Two nurses rushed to the girl's side and held her arms down as a man in a white lab coat appeared. It was Dr. Doug. He plunged a needle into the girl's shoulder. She immediately relaxed, smiling, unaware of the last few hysterical moments.

"Excuse me, but you're not authorized to be here – employees only."

Carla looked up. A stone-faced security guard stared back. She pointed to the monitor. "I was worried about the girl. Is she going to be okay?"

The guard leaned over the counter and turned off the monitor. "We have it under control. You need to leave now."

"But . . ."

"Now."

Carla straightened her jacket and jutted her chin out in a display of indignation as the guard marched her out of the building. Her eyes needed a moment to adjust to the sunlight before recognizing the man leaning against her car with his arms folded. Judah held out his hand, "Keys, please."

Carla took a seat in the back, feeling foolish. "Judah, how did you . . ?"

"Uber. You should try it." He smiled in the rear-view mirror. "Just ask next time, okay? I would have driven you here."

"Sorry. I guess I kind of went crazy back there."

"Have you tried his house?"

"Troy's? No, he's not there."

"Maybe you'll find a clue. Something that will tell you where he is."

"I don't have a key. I couldn't even get past the gate if I wanted to."

Judah arched one eyebrow.

"Oh, no, no, no . . . I can't do that." Carla protested.

"C'mon, it's not like we're going to steal anything. Have a sense of adventure."

Carla waved her hand in the air, "ugh, you're terrible . . . Okay, fine . . . let's do it."

31

The helicopter made a pinpoint landing on the *Gold Star*, a super-yacht 130 meters long with ten decks, three pools, and three Ferrari sports cars for carousing on dry land.

Whitney dared to look down. Not a particularly courageous move since both feet were now firmly planted on the main deck. Nero greeted her, grinning and waving like a happy idiot. An unusual display of confidence for a man about to gamble everything on a puzzle toy, and a nervous red-headed teenager.

Their location, twenty miles off the coast of Los Angeles, was safely situated within international waters. Mr. Chang's people had agreed to let Whitney pay whatever debt she incurred with bitcoins. Whereas, Mr. Chang always paid in cash exactly what Whitney and Nero needed to pull off a con netting $80,000 in a single evening.

A serious looking steward led Whitney and Nero to the ship's lair, a plush lounge area large enough to accommodate fifty guests, although Whitney counted only two dozen men. The scenario had become routine by now. Win or lose, Whitney would hem and haw until her cube opened, freezing everyone in place. She would grab the money and Nero, and be airborne before anyone was the wiser.

The lounge doubled as a disco, with a mirror ball turning above and electronic dance music pumping through hidden speakers. Mr. Chang sat in a leather swivel chair above the dance floor, flanked by armed bodyguards. He wore a blue sport jacket, purple silk shirt, and gold-plated Gucci sunglasses. A potent concoction of sweat and *Axe* body spray clung to the air around him.

Whitney's opponent was a variation on her last

three challengers. A male twenty-something wearing a standard issue hoodie, *Converse* tennis shoes, and a dragon tattoo wrapped around his left eye. He said nothing, hunched over like a teenager forced to eat dinner with his parents.

Nero had come prepared. He hung in the background, holding a pair of sunglasses painted black on the inside. He would slip them on the moment Whitney completed her cube, protecting himself from the stupefying light show.

One of Chang's men stepped forward to do the honors. He held his hand over the table and counted down in a heavy Mandarin accent. Whitney could barely understand him but the inflection in his voice was universal, "On your mark, get set, go!" He dropped his hand and stepped away from the table.

Twenty-five seconds later, Whitney bested her own time, but it wasn't good enough. The creepy arcade guy blew past her, slamming his finished cube down on the table first. As usual the biggest man in the room stepped forward to collect payment. He held an open iPad with a bitcoin interface displayed on the screen. Whitney looked around for Nero. He stood in the background wearing his industrial strength sunglasses, oblivious to the events unfolding. Whitney stalled as best she could, dumpster diving through her purse. She pulled out combs, brushes, a bag of chips, and tampons from the seemingly bottomless bag. Everything but the alleged cheat sheet with her bitcoin security code. The cube was not opening. She had never gotten this far in the act. Everybody should have been stiff as a board by now.

"You know, I think what I really need to do is pee." She pushed her chair away from the table. The big man moved closer, blocking her way. Mr. Chang waved his hand and the bodyguard backed off.

Whitney glanced around looking for the restroom. One of the stewards pointed towards a service door with a small round window. Whitney heard the men grunt disapprovingly as she made her way to the bathroom. She latched the door shut and turned on the sink faucet so they couldn't hear her ranting to herself like a crazy cat lady. She decided to wait a few more minutes before exiting the bathroom, praying the cube would open by then. She bit her lip and pushed. The door flew open, flooding the bathroom with a blinding light show. Whitney shielded her eyes and squinted. The cube had been replaced by a brilliant gaseous orb sucking down the last of the men as music thumped away. A few stragglers hung on to a nearby dance pole, their faces contorted into a cartoonish silent scream as the force pulled their legs like taffy into the abyss. They finally lost their grip, devoured by the light, along with anything not nailed down – including Nero. Whitney looked away, clinging to the wall as she edged sideways towards the exit. She had never been affected by the pull of the light, but this time she could feel its power growing exponentially. She reached a glittering purple door and pushed herself outside on to the main deck. It was a straight shot to the helicopter, revved up and ready to go. A crew member waved for her to board. She felt the force of the cube drawing her backwards. A pair of hands reached out from the open aircraft doors and grabbed her arms, pulling her inside. As the helicopter lifted off she watched the yacht below, turning in circles, pulled under by a magnificent whirlpool. The crew member slammed the helicopter door shut. Whitney yelled over the deafening roar of the aircraft's engine, "What the hell is going on?" The woman slid off her helmet and tossed her hair back as the answer shot from her mouth, "Mission accomplished, sweetheart!"

32

Carla rang the doorbell. No answer. She looked back at Judah sitting in the Land Rover and shrugged her shoulders. He stepped out of the car and walked past her, "Stay here."

A minute later the front door to Troy's house opened. "No one home." Judah smiled, "Come on in." He extended his arm, bowing at the waist.

Carla felt like an intruder stepping over the threshold, "Troy? Hello? It's Carla."

Judah threw his hand up, stopping Carla in her tracks. Whatever she was going to say next caught in her throat. The living room was a shambles. Judah drew his gun, "Stay close behind." Carla did as she was told, hanging on to the back of his jacket as he followed a trail of bloody footprints through the kitchen and into the garage. She kept her distance, watching Judah open the freezer door, his eyes widening. He stood motionless, staring through a swirling white wisp of frigid air. A light dusting of ice crystals melted away, exposing a lump of unwrapped flesh sitting on a platter – a human head, the mouth agape and the eyes cast upwards like a beheaded Goliath.

"What is it?"

Judah slammed the freezer door shut with his foot and slapped a button on the wall. The garage door opened. "Get in the car – now!"

"Judah, you're scaring me. What's in there?"

"I said get in the car!"

Judah grabbed Carla's arm and pulled her down the driveway to the SUV, forcing her into the back seat. She felt something cold and tight around her wrist. She looked down in stunned disbelief as a handcuff snapped into place. Judah secured the other end to a steel bar holding the passenger headrest in place.

"What . . . what the hell are you doing?"

Judah didn't respond. He sat in the driver's seat, his jaw muscles flexing as beads of sweat dripped down the side of his face. He fished something out from under his shirt collar and pushed it into his ear, speaking into his lapel, "I have the girl."

"Oh my god, what's going on? What is this?" Carla yanked on her handcuffs kicking the back of the headrest. She reached across the back seat with her free hand and opened her purse.

"Yeah, go ahead . . . black Mustang . . . got it." Judah punched a string of numbers into his phone. Something cold touched the back of his neck.

"Unlock these now or I swear to god I'll blow your head off."

Judah quickly obliged.

Carla waved him out of the car with her gun, ordering him up against a wrought iron fence. "Here, lock yourself to that." She threw the cuffs at him and stepped back towards the car, snatching his phone off the driver's seat. A flashing blue arrow on the screen pointed to the location of Troy's car. Carla was more angry than scared, "Who the hell are you?"

Judah said nothing.

"What do you want? Money?"

He raised his free hand up in the air as if to surrender, choosing his words carefully, "Look, Carla, you're in a whole lot of trouble. If you stop now, put the gun down . . . you can save yourself."

Carla wasn't listening. She slammed the car door shut and punched the accelerator, spraying Judah with dirt and gravel as she turned on to the road in search of the blue arrow.

33

Jordan never made it to his book signing. He had awakened that morning feeling queasy, his bowel movement the color of lapis lazuli. The cramps and fever subsided by sundown, leaving behind a mild throbbing in his head. He rolled around in bed, his body wrapped in a cocoon of fine Egyptian cotton. Down the road a party raged on, pounding music reverberating through the canyons. He reached for a plastic bottle on the night stand and popped off the top. Dr. Doug's little elves had been hard at work perfecting their antidote for troubled youth. He swallowed the meds with a swig of water and fell back on a pile of pillows, free associating in the dark when a loud crash erupted downstairs. The house alarm beeped three times in quick succession. Somebody was inside.

Jordan snatched an aluminum baseball bat from under his bed and crept down the hallway, peering over the balustrade. The sliding glass door leading to the backyard was wide open. He made his way to the bottom of the stairs, looking down the hallway towards the kitchen. A wet smacking sound drew his attention to the open refrigerator door. An uninvited guest munched on cold pizza. The animal stopped foraging and popped its head up. It had blue eyes, an alkaline nose, and full lips – the face unmistakably human, but the ears long, brown, and covered with fur. "Holy crap!!" Jordan screamed, waving the bat in front of him. The startled creature leaped backward, its hooves slipping and clacking on the tile floor. The two halves did not compute. Above the waist, a naked man, and below a wild buck.

The creature crashed into a rack of pots and pans, scrambling past the kitchen island counter. Jordan chased the animal through the open sliding glass door and out on to the back lawn, watching as it disappeared into the canyon below. He gripped the bat with both hands, his chest heaving. The adrenaline coursing through his veins shook his body, making his breath quiver. The security system had tripped the outdoor lights bathing the lawn in a blue haze. The pool glowed like an aquarium. Jordan stood in place, wound up and ready to strike.

Confident the creature was now long gone, he lowered the bat and breathed more easily. Tomorrow, he would call Dr. Doug to have his prescription changed.

As he turned to face the house something floating in the pool caught his eye. A dark silhouette hovered just below the surface of the water. He moved closer for a better look. The body was so decomposed it barely registered as human, half naked except for a pair of Superman pajama bottoms. He covered his mouth as his stomach flexed, an involuntary reaction to the smell of rotting flesh. He stumbled back into the house and locked the door. His phone vibrated, rattling the glass table top in the dining room. "*Unknown caller*" flashed on the screen. Jordan held the phone to his ear and listened to a vaguely familiar voice.

"They know Jordy."

"Who? What do you mean?"

"They're coming. Get out! Now!"

Jordan ran over to a monitor sitting on the kitchen counter and switched it on. The screen was divided into six different squares, each one a different view of his house. A live video feed of the front porch showed figures dressed in black approaching with guns drawn.

Jordan wasted no time as he flew through the back door, slipping on the wet grass, running down the hill into the canyon. He was shirtless, cold, and barefoot – kicking himself for not grabbing his shoes, and doubly pissed he had left his phone on the dining room table. He blocked out the pain as he ran over pine cones and jagged rocks, ripping through the canyon like a wild animal. He followed the sound of raucous music coming from the party on the other side of the canyon. He could hide there, he thought, blend in with party goers and use someone's phone to call his lawyer. "Rule number one," his lawyer always told him, "Keep your stupid mouth shut until I get there!"

He climbed the canyon wall, grasping at scrub brush and ice plant until he reached the top. He stood on the side of the road a couple hundred yards from the party house, looking back across the canyon where an army of shadowy figures descended upon his yard. A banged up four-door Honda Civic pulled up beside him. A young girl rolled down the window, "Hey Jordan . . . wanna party?"

Jordan looked down at himself, half naked and covered in dirt, wondering how a car full of groupies got past the security gate. He kept walking, only faster now. He looked back at his house. A black SUV was headed his way. He ran up to the Honda and pulled the door open, jumping into the back seat – sandwiched between two screaming teenage girls.

"Alright, alright," Jordan shouted, "be cool or I get out!"

The girl driving looked over her shoulder, "Stop

acting like a little bitch or we'll throw you out!" They all laughed, except Jordan.

One of the girls turned up the music and whipped her head back and forth. Every square inch of their bodies was either tattooed, pierced, shaved, or dyed. Jordan couldn't believe he threw himself to these wolves, but he had no choice. He turned and looked through the rear window, "Hurry up! Can't this piece of shit move any faster?"

The car picked up speed, hugging the curves down the hill, approaching La Fortuna's security gate. A guard emerged from the booth and ran into the middle of the road signaling for them to stop. Jordan leaned forward, shouting over the music into the driver's ear, "I'll give you a five hundred bucks to keep going!"

"A thousand."

"Deal!"

The girls screamed as the car flew past the guard. Jordan looked back in time to see the man dodging flying pieces of metal gate. A few minutes later the Honda raced up an onramp to the 101 Freeway, sweeping across a sea of red tail lights and into the carpool lane, heading east to Hollywood.

The girls passed around a joint, peppering Jordan with questions. He stared straight ahead in a daze, listening to the muffler scrape the asphalt all the way to Sunset Boulevard.

The Honda zig-zagged through the streets of Hollywood, passing a neon sign – *Vine Street Diner*. Jordan pointed, "There, right there! Pull over!" He looked around the back seat, "You guys got a t-shirt or something I can wear?"

"On the floor!" one of the girls yelled.

Jordan sifted through a pile of Starbuck's coffee cups and fast food wrappers, finding a gray sweatshirt with pink paint splattered across the front advertising a yogurt shop. He slipped on a pair of flip-flops and turned to the girl next to him, "Can I borrow those?" He helped himself to her sunglasses. "I'll be back in five minutes. Don't leave without me, alright?"

"Yeah, ok. Just get your sweet ass back here fast – and don't ditch us, we know where you live." The girls laughed and hi-fived each other.

Jordan pushed the car door open and climbed out on to the curb. He spun around and poked his head through the passenger window. "You got any change?" One of the girls dug through the ash tray and gave him a handful of sticky quarters. He turned and entered the diner.

The smell of burgers and fries made Jordan hungry. He scooped up a handful of mint patties from the hostess stand and stuffed them in his mouth, walking to the back of the diner. Mounted on a wall between the restroom doors hung the last pay phone in Los Angeles. Jordan listened for a dial tone before depositing quarters. He suddenly realized he never committed a single phone number to memory. A bell jingled as the diner's front door opened. Jordan looked down the aisle towards the entrance. Two men in business suits and dark glasses entered, scanning the room. One of them flipped open a billfold and held it out to the hostess. She nodded and pointed towards the back of the restaurant where a phone receiver now dangled from its cord. The men reached inside their coats, charging down the aisle.

Jordan locked the restroom door and backed into a stall. He knew he was kidding himself, but it was the only move he had left. A pair of meaty fists banged on the wood door, threatening to smash it to pieces. Jordan covered his ears and braced himself. Just when he thought he couldn't take it anymore the pounding stopped. He no longer heard dishes clanging or waitresses calling out orders – only silence. He stepped out of the stall, faced the locked door, and took a deep breath as he slid the bolt to one side. The door swung open. He steadied himself, extending one foot out to test the plush white carpet with his toes. It was real. His eyes moved across the room verifying the impossible. He was home again.

34

"Let me in dammit! Let me in!" Whitney banged on J.J.'s front door, punching the doorbell over and over, "J.J., it's me! Whitney! Open the goddamn door!" Tears of frustration streamed down her cheeks leaving black trails of mascara. She turned in circles on the welcome mat, not sure what to do next. The door swung open. Furious, Whitney exploded, "It's about time, you asshole!" J.J. turned and headed for the living room. Whitney followed, stepping over potato chip bags and empty cans of diet coke. J.J. sat on the couch, his eyes transfixed on the TV screen. "Hey! J.J.," she snapped her fingers in his face, "my life is falling apart and you're sitting there like a zombie. Didn't you get my messages?

I'm in deep shit J.J. Look at me! What the hell is wrong with you?"

He nodded towards the TV. Whitney looked up at the screen filled with breaking news. A shaken anchorman juggled reports from across the globe as the latest catastrophes unfolded before the cameras. In Paris, Dragellas swooped down, snatching up tourists, and dashing them on the cobblestone streets below – feasting on their entrails. New York, Tokyo, Beijing – millions of people running for their lives in a wave of mass hysteria.

More breaking news splashed across the screen. Somewhere in the middle of the Pacific Ocean, satellites detected a swirling vortex over 800 miles wide, generating tsunamis forty stories high.

Whitney pried her eyes away from the horrific images and looked at J.J., loading a Colt 45 with bullets from a faded cardboard box.

"What are you doing?"

"I'm loading my grandfather's revolver."

"Why?"

"There's something I need to do." He swung the barrel back into place and stood up, staring straight ahead. "I'll be back."

"Wait! Don't leave me alone." She followed behind as J.J. climbed the stairs. "Where are we going?"

J.J. didn't answer. They reached the second floor then climbed another short staircase to the attic door. He turned the knob and in one swift motion pushed it open, swinging his arm upward, pointing the gun at the rafters. Whitney covered her mouth, stifling a scream. J.J. held his position, staring up at a jagged gaping hole in the roof. Ruby had escaped. J.J.'s phone beeped. He pulled it from his pocket and read the GPS alert. Ruby was only yards from the house. He turned and ran down stairs. Whitney followed as he burst through the front door to the outside, aiming the gun up in the air as he spun in circles. There Ruby sat, perched in a pine tree, forty feet up. J.J. fired but missed. Ruby released a primordial screech, launching herself into the air. Her wing span now thirty feet wide. J.J. reached into his pocket and fumbled for his keys, dropping them on the ground. Whitney snatched them up and held them away.

"Give me the keys," J.J. demanded.

Whitney refused, "Not until you listen to me first."

"Dammit Whit! Give me the goddamn keys, now!"

"Alright, but I'm coming with you. There's something you need to know."

35

Harlow found enough space left to squeeze one more thing into her backpack. She looked around her bedroom trying to answer the proverbial question; if the house caught on fire, which single item would she save? There was nothing left of value, at least to her, except the Raggedy-Ann doll and snow globe, both already packed. She slung her arms through the straps of her pink Jub Jub Club backpack and stepped into the hallway, closing the bedroom door behind her. She rubbed her shoulder where Dr. Doug had given her a shot. "That's the last one you'll ever need," he told her, with that creepy neon smile. Harlow had been suspicious of him ever since he showed up at the house, pawing Beverly the way he did. He was a hard truth tolerated as a 'means to an end', a necessary evil that would soon be obsolete. The fact that his chances of survival remained slim at best, gave Harlow a slight lift in her step as she trotted downstairs.

She would miss the house; the way the sun glowed on the wood floors in the late afternoon, the central heat and air that made it impossible to tell the seasons apart, and the wonderful four-star dinners cooked by their very own Cordon Bleu chef. There was a lot to be said for life in La Fortuna, despite its shortcomings.

Harlow paused in the foyer and watched as world events unfolded on a television mounted to the sitting room wall. The President of the United States spoke from behind a podium with a serious tone in his voice. She recognized the golden eagle tie clip, gratified he had taken her advice. He was doing the right thing, she thought, whether he knew it or not.

She turned in place and gazed into the living room for one last look at Beverly and her husband. He had never been around long enough for Harlow to bother learning his name, but his initials were on everything including the towels in the bathroom. She felt kind of sorry for them; Beverly slumped in her chair, covered in vomit, and him on all fours shaking like a dog at the pound, still holding out hope it wasn't the end. The lady was right, Harlow thought, it wasn't too little and it wasn't too much, but just enough to get the job done.

36

Carla pulled to the side of the road. She looked down at Judah's phone. The app indicated Troy's car was parked nearby somewhere. She changed the phone to flashlight mode and held it in front of her, slowly turning in a circle. The light reflected off one of the chrome rims of Troy's car hidden underneath a tarp. Carla walked over and tugged on the canvas cover, exposing the passenger side door. She shined the light through the window. No sign of life. She looked around for clues. The only way through the brush was a path descending into the canyon. A full moon offered just enough light to avoid the larger obstacles as she made her way down to the bottom, walking along the dry creek bed. As she rounded a bend in the path, a sliver of orange light could be seen escaping from the canyon wall. The pump station door had been left open. She stepped inside, calling out, "Troy? Troy are you here?" A musty draft led her to the sliding metal door hidden behind pipes. She stepped into the dimly lit space and waited for her eyes to adjust, "Troy? It's Carla." She proceeded with caution, studying the dark spaces carved out of the sides of the tunnel. Something moved. She screamed and turned, running straight into Troy.

"Carla! It's me. It's okay." Troy shined the flashlight on himself. He wore a park ranger's hat and badge.

"Oh, thank god! It's you." Carla pressed her cheek against his chest, "It's really you!"

Troy smiled from ear to ear, "The lady said you would come!" He took Carla's hand, leading her down the tunnel. She held on to the back of his t-shirt as they stepped further into the dark. Troy reached for a metal box mounted on the wall and flipped one switch after another until the cave flooded with artificial light.

Stalactites, twenty feet in length, hung down from the cavern ceiling – the earthen walls honeycombed with hollowed-out spaces holding hundreds of creatures.

"Oh my god," Carla grabbed Troy with both arms, "What are those things?

"Don't be afraid. It's okay. They're harmless."

"Where did they come from?"

"From us."

Automatic gunfire crackled over their heads, puncturing a perfect row of holes into the cavern wall. Troy pushed Carla to the ground, as bullets whizzed past, pulling her into one of the enclosures. She could see a pair of eyes glowing in the corner. "Oh god! Troy, there's something alive in here!"

"I know, I know, just don't piss it off."

At least half a dozen voices shouted orders back and forth in the dark, quickly closing in.

"Here," Troy took off his necklace and hung it around Carla's neck, "Wear this. It'll protect you." He could see Carla giving in to fear. He held her shoulders, "Look at me. Do what I say and everything will be alright, ok? When I return fire, run as fast as you can in the opposite direction. There's a construction elevator at the end of the tunnel – take it to the top. When you get there, run towards the light. It's the only way out." He could feel her shaking. "You can do it, Carla. I know you can." She believed him because she had to. Troy popped his head out for one last look, "Here we go. Ready? On the count of one, two, three – GO!" Troy rolled out into the open and stood up, spraying bullets into the dark recesses of the cavern. Carla ran as fast as she could towards the elevator but something knocked her down. It was Judah. He wrapped his arm around her neck, pushing a pistol into her back,

"Stop fighting me or I'll shoot goddammit!"

Carla stopped struggling but her muscles remained taught, waiting for a chance to break free. Judah pulled her up off the ground, holding her from behind with his gun jammed into her side. "We're here!" he shouted, "I've got her. I've got the girl!"

A dark figure dressed in camouflage approached them.

"Hurry up goddammit," Judah yelled, "before she chews my arm off!"

The soldier stopped, pointed his gun at Carla, and pulled the trigger. She tried to scream but nothing came out. Judah fell to the ground. Carla looked down at her chest and abdomen. No blood. No wound. The bullet had passed right through her and into Judah who lay stiff and lifeless in the dirt. Her lungs filled with air. She was alive. She was bullet proof.

The soldier took Carla by the arm, "We've got to hurry. They're coming!" He pulled her into the elevator and pushed the button. Carla half fainted, sliding to the floor of the cage as they rose above the sound of gunfire. She felt her body shaking. The soldier pulled a syringe from his vest and jabbed it into her arm. As Carla's senses returned she looked up at the soldier who had removed his hood. He was a she, standing tall and strong with shining emerald eyes. The woman pursed her lips, "Hold on, baby. We're almost there."

The elevator shuttered to a stop. The woman pulled Carla to her feet, sliding the cage door open and pushing her out towards the light. "When you get to the end – jump!"

Carla ran to the end of the tunnel and stood at the edge, looking down at La Fortuna Lake some thirty feet below. She searched for an opening among the black shade balls floating on the surface of the water, took a deep breath, and leapt.

The impact sounded like a clap of thunder, the water rushing past her body with the force of a fire hose. She spread her arms to stop her downward trajectory, kicking off her shoes and swimming to the surface. Wet clothes made it difficult to tread water. She could barely see above the plastic balls, pushing them aside as they broke apart, cracking and popping open, their contents spilling into the lake. The water around her became agitated, bubbling and splashing. An army of creatures with reptilian heads and swishing tails raced alongside her as she swam towards the shore. The creatures continued to grow, sprouting fresh arms and legs, paddling towards the water's edge.

Carla made it to a thin strip of rocky beach and

raced up a steep embankment to the perimeter fence. She looked over her shoulder. The creatures had evolved, trotting out of the water with arms outstretched. They stumbled across the rocks, not yet acclimated to their human bodies – their facial features now fully formed and familiar to Carla. She saw the gardener, and the pool man, and the lady who came once a week to clean her floors – there were hundreds of them.

37

J.J.'s Bentley reached the round-a-bout at the top of the hill and came to a stop.

"He's somewhere right here," Whitney called out. She held J.J.'s phone in her hand, zooming in on the flashing arrow that appeared to be right on top of them. She looked up through the sun roof at an enormous oak tree growing in the middle of the cul-de-sac. "There!" She yelled, "There, up in the tree at three o'clock."

J.J. jumped out of the car with his gun, Although he had no intention of following through with his half-baked plan. He looked up into the expansive canopy. Sitting on a thick arm of the tree, was not one but two Dragellas side by side. Ruby nuzzled the neck of her new friend.

Whitney stood next to J.J., holding his arm. "Look!" she pointed, "There's more."

An endless stream of Dragellas flew overhead. Whitney lowered her gaze and focused on the horizon where the sky met the ocean. A thin silver line stretched across the water, shimmering in the moonlight – a tsunami approached.

J.J.'s shoulders collapsed, "I didn't mean to hurt anyone . . . not Frito's mom, not anyone." He squeezed his eyes shut to keep the tears from coming but they did anyway.

Whitney held him close, "It's okay. Remember what I told you, what the lady said. There's nothing to forgive. We think their thoughts and dream their dreams, but we're not them – not anymore."

38

Jordan sat on the leather couch facing the sliding glass doors to his backyard. He wasn't sure what to do next. He closed his eyes and tried meditating. Something softly beeped. He embraced the rhythm, drifting towards a higher plane.

"It's time, Jordy."

He opened his eyes. Brandon stood before him wearing his Eagle Scout uniform – a sash draped across his chest, covered in merit badges. Jordan wanted to explain, beg his brother for forgiveness, but there was no time. Brandon lifted his arm and pointed to the corner of the room.

"Pick it up, Jordy."

Jordan obeyed his brother's command, walking towards a flashing red light on the floor. He took the remote control into his hands and studied it more closely. It was the same one he had tossed aside. The one Brandon had used to fly the drone. The one he had placed in the time capsule hoping to never see again. Jordan looked up. Brandon was standing at the back door, signaling his brother to follow.

They stood together, looking out over the valley. The lights below formed a grid of red and white dotted lines along the boulevards. In the middle was a dark mass where the shuttered military base stood. Jordan held the remote up in the air with both hands, scanning the horizon as the beeps drew closer together – becoming a single tone. The light turned green, the target locked in. Jordan pressed the button with his right thumb. A loud boom followed a flash of brilliant light in the distance. The missile emerged from its silo and shot into the sky, tilting towards the Pacific Ocean. Jordan felt a rush of wonder. Who knew such a thing still lurked below. An artifact from an era gone by, a messenger of what was to come.

Where Are They Now?

39

Carla stopped at the top of the incline to catch her breath, glancing back at the lake – the surface smooth and undisturbed. The cool night air sent a chill through her body. Wet and naked, she drew her arms against her chest and followed the shortest path home – across a field of dried mustard flowers and through a neighbor's yard. She grabbed a beach towel hanging from a chaise lounge and covered herself. Less than a mile and she would be home. Once there, she would regroup and try to remember what it was she needed to remember – start from the beginning and retrace her steps until everything made sense.

She entered her property through a rear gate, walking past the black-bottom pool, and climbing the hill to her house. She opened one of the French doors and stepped into the living room. A single table lamp shined down on a steaming cup of hot tea. It was quiet, almost too quiet. Things looked different; a stack of books she didn't recognize, a painting where there had been none, and her music box sitting on the fireplace mantle. She approached the childhood keepsake and lifted the lid. Adam and Eve sprang up, dancing to a Vienna Waltz, as the bottom drawer slid open. It was empty.

"They always go for the gun first."

Carla spun around. An old woman held the Fabulizer in her hand. It was no longer shiny or new.

"It's ok." The woman told Carla, "You can't help it. It's in your nature."

The woman leaned on a cane, the right side of her face drooping slightly, her white hair tied back into a loose knot. She wore a floral print nightgown and Terri-cloth slippers. The hand holding the gun shook more than just a little.

Carla was so cold she could barely speak. "Who are you? Why are you here?"

"This is my home." The woman replied.

Carla tightened the towel around her shivering frame, "I . . . I must be in the wrong place."

"No honey," the woman's voice softened, "you're exactly where you should be." She kept the gun trained on Carla as she sat on a dining chair, surrounded by an assortment of empty water glasses and pill bottles. "My god," she marveled, "you really are beautiful, aren't you?" She gazed at Carla for a moment, before waving the gun in the air, "See that folded piece of plastic on the table over there? I want you to spread it out over the carpet."

"Why?"

"Just do it, dear."

Carla followed orders, unfolding the six by six-foot sheet of plastic, and laying it down in the center of the room.

"Now, if you would please stand in the middle."

the old lady directed.

Carla's feet stuck to the plastic as she tiptoed to the center and stood in place. The woman noticed Carla staring at the gun, "I'm so sorry dear, but it really is necessary. You see, it wasn't long ago the mere sight of my face would have sent you into a murderous rage. Of course, Mother Nature threw a monkey wrench into all that, didn't she? Me an old woman now, and you the young Carla Shane. I guess for once, time is finally on my side.

"I don't understand. What happened?"

"One of you shot me and left me for dead on a bathroom floor, that's what happened - at least, that's what they told me. I was in a coma for six weeks, missed the whole thing. Woke up to people dancing in the streets."

Carla tried to remember how she got home but her head hurt too much. The woman continued talking but nothing made sense. "You need to stop." Carla's voice quivered, "You need to leave my house now, or I'll call security." She looked past the old woman. "Where's my mother? Where's Dina?"

"She's gone dear, they're all gone."

Carla tried to cover her mouth but it was too late. A blue liquid forced its way between her fingers, dripping down her chin and splattering on to the floor. The old woman averted her eyes, "It's the chemicals they put in the lake. It usually does the job, but every so often, one of you manage to make it to the house – convinced you are whoever you think you are. It's a miracle any of you make it this far."

A burning sensation shot up Carla's spine and spread to her extremities. Her arms flailed and legs buckled as she crumbled to the floor. The pungent odor of burning protein filled the room. Something covered in blue shimmering scales spilled out of her, flopping around on the floor until it finally expired.

The old woman laid the gun down on the table and watched as the last of Carla bubbled away, leaving a bitter residue on the plastic sheet. She paused for a moment to say a little prayer before pushing herself upright with the help of her cane. The unexpected visitor had worn her out. It wasn't every day one came face to face with the enemy. The old woman slowly shuffled down the hall. It was time for bed. The maid would clean up in the morning.

The End

About the Author

Kingston Crow is a writer and illustrator living in Los Angeles, California. Keep up with the author's latest news, books, and projects by visiting kingstoncrow.com. Sign-up for the Newsletter and receive information about upcoming books, exclusive offers, and more.

kingstoncrow.com